The Life of
Stephen A. Douglas

William Gardner

Contents

THE LIFE OF
STEPHEN A. DOUGLAS

BY

William Gardner

Preface.

De mortuis nil nisi bonum, (of the dead speak nothing but good), is the rule which governed the friends of Stephen A. Douglas after his death. "Of political foes speak nothing but ill," is the rule which has guided much of our discussion of him for forty years. The time has now arrived when we can study him dispassionately and judge him justly, when we can take his measure, if not with scientific accuracy, at least with fairness and honesty.

Where party spirit is as despotic as it is among us, it is difficult for any man who spends his life amid the storms of politics to get justice until the passions of his generation have been forgotten. Even then he is generally misjudged--canonized as a saint, with extravagant eulogy, by those who inherit his party name, and branded as a traitor or a demagogue by those who wear the livery of opposition.

Douglas has perhaps suffered more from this method of dealing with our political heroes than any other American statesman of the first class. He died at the opening of the Civil War. It proved to be a revolution which wrought deep changes in the character of the people. It was the beginning of a new era in our national life. We are in constant danger of missing the real worth of men in these ante-bellum years because their modes of thought and feeling were not those of this generation.

The Civil War, with its storm of passion, banished from our minds the great men and gigantic struggles of the preceding decade. We turned with scornful impatience from the pitiful and abortive compromises of those times, the puerile attempts to cure by futile plasters the cancer that was eating the vitals of the nation. We hastily concluded that men who belonged to the party of Jefferson Davis and Judah P. Benjamin during those critical years were of doubtful loyalty and questionable patriotism, that men who battled with Lincoln, Seward and Chase could hardly be true-hearted lovers of their country. Douglas died too soon to make clear to a passion-stirred world that he was as warmly attached to the Union, as intensely loyal, as devotedly patriotic, as Lincoln himself.

The grave questions arising from the War, which disturbed our politics for twenty years, the great economic questions which have agitated us for the past fifteen years, bear slight relation to those dark problems with which Douglas and his contemporaries grappled. He was on the wrong side of many struggles preliminary to the War. He was not a profound student of political economy, hence is not an authority for any party in the perplexing questions of recent times. The result is that the greatest political leader of the most momentous decade of our history is less known to us than any second-rate hero of the Revolution.

It is not of much importance now to any one whether Douglas is loved or hated, admired or despised. It is of some importance that he be understood.

I have derived this narrative mainly from original sources. The biography written during his life-time by his friend Sheahan, and that published two years after his death by his admirer, Flint, are chiefly drawn on for the brief account of his early life. The history of his career in Congress has been gathered from the Congressional record; the account of Conventions from contemporary reports, and the Debates with Lincoln from the authorized publication.

I have not consciously taken any liberty with any text quoted, except to omit superfluous words, which omissions are indicated by asterisks. I have not attempted to pronounce judgement on Douglas or his contemporaries, but to submit the evidence. Not those who write, but those who read, pass final judgement on the heroes of biography.

Chapter I. Youth.

Stephen Arnold Douglas was born at Brandon, Vermont, on the 23rd of April, 1813. His father was a physician, descended from Scotch ancestors, who had settled in Connecticut before the Revolution. his mother was the daughter of a prosperous Vermont farmer. Before he was three months old his father, whose only fortune was his practice, suddenly died. A bachelor brother of the widow took the family to his home near Brandon, where they lived for fifteen years. When not needed at more important work Stephen attended the common school. but the serious business of life was tilling his uncle's fields.

At fifteen he sought help to prepare for college. His uncle declined to assume the burden of his education and advised him to shun the perils of professional life and adopt the safe and honorable career of a farmer. The advice was rejected and he obtained permission to earn his way and shape his future. He walked to Middlebury, a distance of fourteen miles, and apprenticed himself to a cabinet maker. He worked with energy and enthusiasm, became a good mechanic and bade fair to win success at his trade, but owning to delicate health he abandoned the shop after less than two years' service, and entered the academy at Brandon, where he pursued his studies for about a year, when his mother married again and moved to Canandiagua, New York. He there entered an academy and continued an industrious student for nearly three years, devoting part of his time to law study. This ended his preliminary training. He quit the schools and applied himself to the work of practical life.

In June, 1833, he left home to push his fortune in the West. His health was delicate, his stock of money scant. He went to Cleveland, Ohio, where he became acquainted with a lawyer named Andrews, who, pleased with the appearance of the youth, invited him to share his office and use his library, with the promise of a partnership when admitted to the bar. The offer was accepted and he began his duties as law clerk. A week later he was taken seriously sick, and at the end of his long illness the doctors advised him to return home. He rejected the advice and in October took passage on a canal boat for Portsmouth, on the Ohio river, and went thence to Cincinnati. For a week he sought employment. Unable to find it he went to Louisville, where another week was spent in vain quest of work. He continued his journey to St. Louis, where he landed in the late autumn. An eminent lawyer offered him free use of his library, but an empty purse compelled him to decline the offer and seek immediate work. He went to Jacksonville, Illinois, arriving late in November, and addressed himself to the pressing problem of self-support. The remnant of his cash amount to thirty-seven cents.

Chapter II. Apprenticeship.

In those days Illinois was a frontier State with about 200,000 population, chiefly settled in its southern half. A large part of the people were from the South and, in defiance of the law, owned many negro slaves. The Capital was at Vandalia, although Jacksonville and Springfield were the towns of highest promise and brightest prospects. Chicago contained a few score of people to whom the Indians were still uncomfortably close neighbors. Railroads and canals were beginning to be built, with promise of closer relations between the villages and settlements theretofore lost in the solitudes.

Finding no employment at Jacksonville, he sold his few books to keep off hunger and walked to Winchester. On the morning after his arrival he found a crowd assembled on the street where a public sale was about to open. Delay was occasioned by the want of a competent clerk and he was hired for two dollars a day to keep the record of the sale. He was then employed to teach a private school in the town at a salary of forty dollars a month. Besides teaching he found time to read a few borrowed law books and try an occasional case before the village justice.

Having been admitted to the bar in March, 1834, he opened a law office at Jacksonville. His professional career, though successful, was so completely eclipsed by the brilliancy of his political achievements that it need not detain us. The readiness and agility of his mind; the adaptability of his convictions to the demands of the hour; his self-confident energy, were such that he speedily developed into a good trial lawyer and won high standing at the bar. That the profession was not then as lucrative as it has since become, is evidenced by the fact that he traveled from Springfield to Bloomington and argued a case for a fee of five dollars.

But his time and energy were devoted to politics rather than law. The strategy of parties interested him more than Coke or Justinian. Jacksonville was a conservative, religious town, whose population consisted chiefly of New England Puritans and Whigs. But the prairies were settled by a race of thoroughly Democratic pioneers to whom the rough victor at New Orleans was a hero in war and a master in statecraft.

Douglas was an enthusiastic Democrat and an ardent admirer of President Jackson. The favorite occupation of the young lawyer, not yet harassed by clients, was to talk politics to the farmers, or gather them into his half furnished office and discuss more gravely the questions of party management.

A few days after his arrival the opportunity came to distinguish himself in the field of his future achievements. A mass meeting was called at the court house for the purpose of endorsing the policy of the President in removing the deposits of public money from the United States bank and vetoing the bill for its recharter. The opposition was bitter. In the state of public temper it was a delicate task to present the resolutions. The man who had undertaken it lost courage at the sight of the multitude and handed them to Douglas, and the crowd looked with amused surprise when the young stranger, who was only five feet tall, appeared on the platform. He read the resolutions of endorsement and supported them in a brief speech.

When he sat down, Josiah Lamborn, an old and distinguished lawyer and politician, attacked him and the resolutions in a speech of caustic severity. Douglas rose to reply. The people cheered the plucky youngster. The attack had sharpened the faculties and awakened his fighting courage. He had unexpectedly found the field of action in which he was destined to become an incomparable master. For an hour he poured out an impassioned harangue, without embarrassment or hesitation. Astonishment at what seemed a quaint freak soon gave way to respect and admiration, and at the close of this remarkable address the hall and courtyard rang with loud applause. The excited crowed seized the little orator, lifted him on their shoulders and bore him in triumph around the square.

The young adventurer in the fields of law and politics was thenceforth a man of mark--a man to be reckoned with in Illinois. There were scores of better lawyers and more eminent politicians in the State, but a real leader, a genuine master of men had appeared.

In January, 1835, the legislature met at Vandalia. Early in the session it elected

Douglas State's Attorney of the First Judicial District--an extraordinary tribute to the professional or political ability of the young lawyer of less than a year's standing. He held the office a little more than a year and resigned to enter the legislature.

This was a really memorable body. Among its members were James Shields, afterwards United States Senator, John Calhoun of Lecompton fame, W. A. Richardson, afterwards Democratic leader in the House of Representatives, John A. McClernand, destined also to distinguish service in Congress and still more distinguished service as a major general and rival in arms of Grant and Sherman, Abraham Lincoln, an awkward young lawyer, from Springfield, and Douglas, whose fate it was to give Lincoln his first national prominence and then sink eclipsed by the rising glory of his great rival. The only memorable work of the session was the removal of the Capital from Vandalia to Springfield, and the authorization of twelve millions of debt, to be contracted for government improvements.

Douglas, who had opposed these extravagant appropriations, having distinguished himself as a debater, an organizer and a leader, was, a few days after the adjournment, appointed Register of the United States Land Office at Springfield, to which place he at once removed.

In the following November he was nominated for Congress. The district, which included the entire northern part of the State, was large enough for an empire, with sparse population and wretched means of communication. The campaign lasted nine months, during which, having resigned the office of the Register, he devoted himself to the task of riding over the prairies, interviewing the voters and speaking in school houses and village halls. The monotony was relieved by the society of the rival candidate, John T. Stuart, who as Lincoln's law partner. Stuart was declared elected by a doubtful majority of five, and Douglas, after soothing his wounded feelings by apparently well founded charges of an unfair count and threats of a contest, abandoned it in disgust and returned to his law office. He announced his determination to quit politics forever.

But in December, 1838, the legislature began a session at the old Capital. The Governor declared the office of Secretary of State vacant and appointed John A. McClernand to fill it. Field, the incumbent, questioned the power of the Governor to remove him and declined to surrender the office. Quo warranto proceedings were instituted by McClernand, with Douglas and others as counsel. The Supreme Court denied the Governor's power of removal. The Court became involved in the parti-san battle which raged with genuine Western fervor for two years.

In the early weeks of 1841, a bill was passed, reorganizing the Judiciary, pro-viding for the election by the legislature of five additional Supreme Judges, and imposing the duties of trial Judges upon the members of the Court. Meanwhile, Field had grown weary of the struggle with a hostile Governor and legislature, and, being threatened with a sweeping change of the Court, resigned in January, 1841. The Governor appointed Douglas his successor. Five weeks later the legislature chose him Justice of the Supreme Court and presiding Judge of the Fifth District. He resigned the office of Secretary and began his judicial career, establishing his residence at Quincy.

This appointment to the bench was one of the most fortunate incidents in his busy and feverish life. He was not twenty-eight years old. Adroit, nimble-witted and irrepressibly energetic as he was, he had not yet developed much solid strength. His stock of knowledge was scanty and superficial. From force of circumstances he had devoted little time to calm thought or serious study. Early convinced that all truth lay on the surface, patent to him who had eyes to see, he had plunged into the storm of life and, by his aggressive and overmastering energy, had conquered a place for himself in the world. He was an experienced politician, a famous cam-paign orator, and a Justice of the Supreme Court at a period when most boys are awkwardly finding their way into the activities of the world. The younger Pitt was Chancellor of the Exchequer at twenty-three; but he was the son of Chatham, nurtured in statesmanship from the cradle. the younger Adams was Minister to the Hague at twenty-five; but he was already a ripe scholar and heir to his father's great fame. Douglas was a penniless adventurer, a novus homo, with none of those ac-cidents of fortune which sometimes give early success to gifted men.

The opportunity afforded the young Judge to extend his knowledge and mingle on terms of equality with the masters of his profession was such as rarely falls to the lot of a half-educated man of twenty-eight. He did not become an eminent Judge, yet he left the bench, after three years' service, with marked improvement in the solidity and dignity of his character.

Chapter III. Member of Congress.

The legislature met in December, 1842, to chose a Senator. Douglas still lacked six months of the thirty years required, but came within five votes of the election.

In the following spring he received the Democratic nomination for Congress and resigned his judgeship to enter the campaign. The District included eleven large counties in the western part of the State. O. H. Browning of Quincy, a lawyer of ability, destined to a distinguished political career and to succeed to Douglas' vacant seat in the Senate twenty years later, was the Whig candidate. They held a long series of joint discussions, addressed scores of audiences and so exhausted themselves that both were prostrated with serious sickness after the campaign. The questions discussed are as completely obsolete as the political issues of the antediluvians. Douglas was elected by a small majority.

He was in Washington at the opening of Congress and entered upon his eventful and brilliant career on that elevated theatre, though he was as yet only the crude material out of which a statesman might be evolved. He was a vigorous, pushing Western politician, with half developed faculties and vague, unlimited ambition, whose early congressional service gave small promise of the great leader of after years.

The famous description of him contained in the Adams diary relates to this period of his life. The venerable ex-President, then a Member of the House, mentions him as the homunculus Douglas and with acrid malevolence describes him as raving out his hour in abusive invectives, his face convulsed, his gesticulation frantic, and lashing himself into such heat that if his body had been made of combustible matter it would have burned out.

"In the midst of his roaring," he declares, "to save himself from choking, he stripped off and cast away his cravat, unbuttoned his waistcoat and had the air and aspect of a half-naked pugilist." With all its extravagance and exaggeration, it is impossible to doubt the substantial truth of this charicature. Adams did not live to see the young Member become the most powerful debater, the most accomplished political leader and most influential statesman of the great and stirring period that ensued.

The time was strange, as difficult of comprehension to the generation that has grown up since the War as the England of Hengist and Horsa is to the modern Cockney, or the Rome of Tiberius to the present inhabitant of the Palentine Hill. Only sixty years have passed, but with them has passed away civilization, with its modes of thought and sentiment, its ethics and its politics. The country had but one fifth of its present population. A third of our area was still held by Mexico. Wealth was as yet the poet's dream or the philosopher's night-mare. Commerce was a subordinate factor in our civilization. Agriculture was the occupation of the people and the source of wealth. Cotton was king not only in the field of business, but in that of politics. The world still maintained its attitude of patronizing condescension or haughty contempt toward the dubious experiment of "broad and rampant democracy." Dickens had just written his shallow twaddle about Yankee crudeness and folly. Macaulay was soon to tell us that our Constitution was "all sail and no anchor." DeTocqueville had but recently published his appreciative estimate of the New World civilization. Americans knew they had less admiration than they claimed and had lurking doubts that there was some ground for the ill-concealed contempt of the Old World toward the swaggering giant of the New, and a fixed resolve to proclaim their supreme greatness with an energy and persistence that would drown the sneers of all Europe. It was a time of egotism, bluster and brag in our relation to the foreign world, and of truckling submission in our home politics to a dominant power, long since so completely whirled away by the storm of revolution, that it is hard to realize that half a century ago the strongest bowed to its will.

Douglas was in no sense a reformer or the preacher of a crusade. He was ready to cheerfully accept the ethics of the time without criticism or question. Political morality was at its nadir. The dominant power of slavery was not alone responsible for this depravity. The country was isolated from the world and little influenced by foreign thought. Its energies were devoted to material aggrandizement, to the conquest of Nature on a gigantic scale, to the acquisition of wealth. Since the settlement of the Constitution moral problems had dropped out of political life and the great passions of the heroic age had died away. Education was superficial. Religion was emotional and spasmodic. Business ethics was low.

Party politics was in a chaotic condition. The Whig organization was not in any proper sense a party at all. It was an ill-assorted aggregation of political elements, without common opinions or united purposes, whose only proper function was opposition. It was so utterly incoherent, its convictions so vague and negative, that it was unable even to draft a platform. Without any formal declaration of principles or purposes it had nominated and elected Harrison and Tyler, one a distinguished soldier and respectable Western politician, the other a renegade Virginia Democrat, whose Whiggism consisted solely of a temporary quarrel with his own party. The one unanimous opinion of the party was that it was better for themselves, if not for the country, that the Whigs should hold the offices. The Democrats had been in control of the Government for forty years. Their professed principles were still broadly Jeffersonian. Their platform consisted mainly of a denial of all power in the Federal Government to do anything or prevent anything, the extravagant negations borrowed from the republican philosophers of England and the French Revolutionists.

But a half century of power had produced a marked diversion of practice from principles, and, in spite of its open abnegation of power, the Government had become a personal despotism under Jackson, which had vainly struggled to perpetuate itself through the Administration of VanBuren. But notwithstanding the absurd discrepancy of their practical and theoretical politics, the Democrats had one great advantage over the Whigs in having a large and influential body of men united in interest, compelled to defend themselves against aggression, prepared unflinchingly to take the initiative, to whom politics was not a philosophic theory but a serious matter of business.

The slave-holding aristocracy of the South was the only united, organized, positive political force in the country. With the personal tastes of aristocrats and the domestic habits of despots, they were staunchly Democratic in their politics and had full control of the party. They had positive purposes and aggressive courage. A crisis had come which they only had the ability and energy to meet. The control of affairs was in the hands of the timid Whigs. Decisive measures were needed. By a peaceful revolution they seized the Government out of the hands of the Whigs in the midst of the Administration and embarked on a career of Democratic conquest.

President Tyler, having quarreled with his party, eager to accomplish something striking in the closing hours of his abortive Administration, with unseemly haste rushed through the annexation of Texas under a joint resolution of Congress. Mr. Polk, the new President, did not hesitate in carrying out the manifest will of the people and the imperious behest of his party. The South was clamoring for more territory for the extension of slavery. The West was aggressive and eager for more worlds to conquer. New England, impelled by hatred of slavery and jealousy of the rising importance of the West, opposed the entire project and earnestly protested against annexation.

In the feverish dreams of the slavery propagandists rose chimerical projects of conquest and expansion at which a Caesar or an Alexander would have stood aghast. Mexico and Central America were contemplated as possible additions to the magnificent slave empire which they saw rising out of the mists of the future. They began to talk of the Caribbean Sea as an inland lake, of Cuba and the West Indies as outlying dependencies, of the Pacific as their western coast, and of the States that should thereafter be carved out of South America. The enduring foundation of this tropical empire was to be African slavery, and the governing power was to rest permanently in the hands of a cultured aristocracy of slave-holders. The people of the North-Atlantic States and heir descendents in the Northwest, who churlishly held aloof from these intoxicating dreams, were to be treated with generous justice and permitted to go in peace or continue a minor adjunct of the great aristocratic Republic. Already the irrepressible conflict had begun.

Douglas heartily accepted the plans of his party. He was by temperament an ardent expansionist, a firm believer in the manifest destiny of his country to rule the Western Continent, a pronounced type of exuberant young Americanism. He was an unflinching partisan seeking to establish himself in the higher councils of his party, which was committed to this scheme of conquest. On May 13th, 1846, he delivered in the House a speech, in which he defended the course of the Administration in regard to the Mexican War and, in a spirited colloquy, instructed the venerable John Quincy Adams in the principles of international law. He based his defense of the war upon the treaty with Santa Anna recognizing the independence of Texas. Adams suggested that at the time of its execution Santa Anna was a prisoner incapable of making a treaty. Douglas insisted that, even though a captive, he was a de facto government whose acts were binding upon the country, and to establish his proposition cited the case of Cromwell who, during his successful usurpation, bound England by many important treaties. The niceties of international law were not very punctiliously observed. His arguments were warmly received by men already resolved on a career of conquest.

The war was a romantic military excursion through the heart of Mexico. There were battles between the triumphant invaders and the demoralized natives, which were believed entitled to rank among the supreme achievements of genius and courage. Americans had not yet acquired that deep knowledge of carnage, those stern conceptions of war, which they were destined soon to gain. Military glory and imperial conquest have rarely been so cheaply won. The war gave enduring fame to the commanding generals and shed a real luster over the lives of thousands of men.

The material results were stupendous. We acquired nearly twelve hundred thousand square miles of territory--a region one-third larger than the area of the United States at the close of the Revolution. The extravagant dream of making the Pacific the western boundary of the Republic was realized and no one seriously doubted that this vast domain was surrendered to slavery.

Chapter IV. The Compromise of 1850.

Douglas served two terms in the House and was again elected in 1846, but in January following was chosen Senator, taking his seat on March 4th, 1847. In April following he married Martha Denny Martin, daughter of a wealthy North Carolina planter and slave-owner.

The Senate, during the early years of his service, was in its intellectual gifts altogether the most extraordinary body ever assembled in the United States. Rarely, if ever, in the history of the world, have so many men of remarkable endowment, high training and masterful energy been gathered in a single assembly. It was the period when the generation of Webster, Clay and Calhoun overlapped that of Seward, Chase and Sumner, when the men who had set at the feet of the Revolutionary Fathers and had striven to settle the interpretation of the Constitution met the men who were destined to guide the Nation through the Civil War and settle the perplexing questions arising from it.

Webster was now an old man, his face deep lined with care, disappointment and dissipation. Though sixty-eight years old and the greatest orator of the century, his heart was still consumed with unquenchable thirst of the honor of succeeding John Tyler and James K. Polk. Calhoun, now sixty-five years old, a ghastly physical wreck, still represented South Carolina and dismally speculated on the prospect of surviving the outgrown Union. Cass, equal in years with Calhoun, still held his seat in the Senate and cherished the delusive hope of yet reaching the Presidency. Benton was closing his fifth and last term in the Senate, and Clay, the knightly leader of the trimming Whigs, though now in temporary retirement, was soon to return and resume his old leadership.

Within the first four years of Douglas' service, Salmon P. Chase, William H. Seward and Charles Sumner made their appearance in the Senate. A new generation of giants seemed providentially supplied as the old neared the end of their service. Douglas, though serving with both these groups of statesmen, belonged to neither. Running his career side by side with the later school of political leaders and sharing in the great struggles on which their fame, in large part, rests, his character and ideals were those of the older generation.

The questions confronting Congress were of transcendent interest and incalculable importance. A sudden and astounding expansion had occurred, calling for the highest, wisest and most disinterested statesmanship in providing governments for the newly acquired domain. A million and a half miles of new territory, extending through sixteen degrees of latitude, was now to be organized; the future destiny of this vast territory, and indirectly that of free institutions generally, was supposed to depend on the decision of Congress. Above all, the fate of the American apple of discord, human slavery, was understood to be involved in the construction of territorial and State governments for these new possessions. It was deemed by the South indispensable to the safety and permanence of slavery to plant it in them.

For that half-disguised purpose they had been acquired at great expense of blood and money. New States, it was hoped, might now be created south of the line below which slavery flourished, balancing those to be admitted from the growing Northwest. Thus far the adventurous West had powerfully supported the South in its schemes of conquest, but had no sympathy with slavery. The old North, thought ready to submit to its continued existence in the States where already established, was implacably hostile to its further spread.

It was not a question of ethics or of sober statesmanship, but one of practical politics, that divided the North and the South at this period. Each hoped to secure for itself the alliance and sympathy of the new States thereafter admitted. Each applied itself to the task of shaping the Territories and moulding the future States to serve its ulterior views.

When Congress attempted to organize territorial governments, the people of the North insisted on the exclusion of slavery from Oregon and the territory acquired from Mexico. The people of the South made no resistance to its exclusion from Oregon. It was already excluded by "the ordinance of Nature or the will of God." But that the vast territory torn from Mexico, acquired by the common blood and treasure, should now be closed to their institution, was intolerable. To secure it they had sinned deep. After the conquest their position was peculiarly awkward. The laws of Mexico excluding slavery continued in force. Hence in all this territory slavery was as effectually prohibited as in Massachusetts until Congress could accomplish the odious work of introducing it by express enactment. Calhoun strenuously argued the novel proposition that, on the overthrow of the authority of the Mexican government by American arms, the laws and constitution of Mexico were extinguished and those of the United States, so far as applicable, occupied the vacant field; that the Federal Constitution carried slavery with it wherever it went, except where by the laws of a sovereign State it was excluded.

He announced the proposition afterwards established by the Supreme Court, that, as the Constitution proprio vigore carried slavery into all the Territories, neither the territorial legislatures nor Congress itself had power to interfere with the right of holding slaves within them.

Webster conclusively answered this refined sophistry, pointing out that slavery was merely a municipal institution, in derogation of the common right of mankind, against the native instincts of humanity, dependent wholly for its right of existence upon local legislation, and that the real demand of the people of the South was not to carry their slaves into the new Territories, but to carry with them the slave codes of their several States.

While the venerable leaders who had ruled Congress and swayed public opinion for thirty years were uttering philosophic disquisitions on constitutional law or the ethics of slavery, Douglas had with practical sagacity offered an amendment to the Oregon bill, extending the line of the Missouri Compromise to the Pacific. This would not decide the great moral question between those who believed slavery an unmixed good and those who believed it the sum of all villainies. But he thought that moral ideas had no place in politics. It would not decide the great question of constitutional law between those who, like Calhoun, believed slavery the creature of the Federal Constitution, and those, who, like Webster, believed it the creature of local municipal law. But it promised a temporary respite to the vexed question. He had already, in the House, advocated the extension of this line through the Western Territories. He believed that adhesion to this venerable Compromise, now as sacred as the Constitution itself, was the hope of the future and succeeded in persuading the Senate to adopt his amendment as the final solution of the vexed problem. It was rejected in the House and the question indefinitely postponed.

In the Territories, meanwhile, events moved fast. While Congress had been wrangling over the new possessions, gold was discovered in California. A tumultuous rush of people, unparalleled since the Crusades, at once began by all routes from every region to the new El Dorado. More than 80,000 settlers arrived in 1849. A spontaneous movement of the people resulted in a Constitutional Convention, which met at Monterey on September 3d of that year, and adopted a Constitution which forever prohibited slavery. It was submitted to a vote and adopted in November.

Congress met on December 3d and resumed the Sisyphean labors of the last session. Douglas was chairman of the Committee on Territories, to which were referred all measures affecting the recent acquisitions--altogether the most momentous of the session--which stirred the deepest passions of Congress and held the keenest attention of the people. In the early days of December he submitted to his Committee two bills. One provided for the immediate admission of California; the other for the establishment of governments for Utah and New Mexico and the adjustment of the Texas boundary. On March 25th they were reported to the Senate. Meanwhile Taylor, in a special message, had recommended the immediate admission of California. Senator Mason had introduced a bill providing more effective means for the summary return of fugitive slaves, in effect converting the population of the free States into a posse comitatus charged with the duty of hunting down the fugitive sand returning him to bondage. The clash of arms had begun. Both sides were passionately in earnest and resolved to encounter the utmost extremity rather than yield. The Democrats had a small majority in the Senate, while in the House neither party had a majority.

The Free Soilers held the balance of power, but by a refusal to cooperate with the conservative opponents of slavery extension left the control of the House in the hands of the Democrats. The chief business of the early weeks of the session was the delivery of defiant speeches and the presentation of resolutions defining the opinions of various segments of distracted parties and revealing the chasm that was opening between the friends and opponents of slavery.

On the 21st of January the rival Whig chiefs of the Senate held a confidential conference. Clay submitted a plan of compromise covering the whole field of controversy. Webster promised his cordial support. A week later Clay presented the first draft of his famous slavery Compromise. He was under the sincere illusion that he had been spared by Providence that he might save his country in this great exigency and that his bill would secure long years of peace and harmony. At least, as many of them were old men, it would postpone the evil day until they had been safely gathered to their fathers, and, according to the political morals of the age, the next generation must take care of itself. Douglas moved to refer the resolutions to the Committee on Territories; but, on motion of Foote of Mississippi, they were referred to a select Committee of Thirteen, consisting of three Northern Whigs, three Southern Whigs, three Southern and three Northern Democrats, with Clay as chairman. Douglas was not on this Committee. It was composed of old Senators whose established reputations were expected to give credit to any proposition of compromise.

On May 8th the Committee reported, recommending the immediate admission of California, the establishment of territorial governments in New Mexico and Utah with no mention of the slavery question, the settlement of the Texas boundary dispute and the enactment of a law providing for the more effectual return of fugitive slaves. Substantially it was Douglas' two bills joined together, with Mason's Fugitive Slave bill annexed. It was a mass of unrelated measures, jumbled together for the illegitimate purpose of compelling support of the whole from friends of the several parts.

Clay spoke for two days in support of his great masterpiece of compromising statesmanship. He insisted that it should be accepted by all for the reason that "neither party made any concession of principle, but only of feeling and sentiment," and ingeniously sought to soothe the anger of the North by the assurance that the principle of popular sovereignty embodied in the bill was not only eminently just and in harmony with the spirit of our institutions but entirely harmless, inasmuch as the North had Nature on its side, facts on its side and the truth staring it in the face that there was no slavery in the Territories, proving that the law of Nature was of paramount force.

On March 4th Calhoun attempted to speak, but found himself unable and handed his speech to Mason who read it for him. He rejected Clay's Compromise as futile and denied utterly the right of the inhabitants of a Territory to exclude slavery. He accused the North of having pursued a course of systematic hostility to Southern institutions since the close of the Revolution, and cited the Ordinance of 1787, the Missouri Compromise and the exclusion of slavery from Oregon as instances of Northern aggression; and now, he said, the final and fatal act of exclusion was attempted. He denounced the action of the people of California in organizing a State without congressional authority as revolutionary and rebellious. He grimly announced that the South had no concessions to make, even to save the poor wreck of a once glorious Union. He plainly told them that if the Union was to be saved the North must save it. It must open the Territories to slavery. It must surrender fugitive slaves. It must cease agitating the slavery question. The Constitution must be amended so as to restore to the South the power of protecting itself. If they were not willing to do these acts of justice, nor that the South should depart in peace, let them say so, that it might know what to do when the question was reduced to one of submission or resistance.

Three days later Webster delivered his famous 7th of March speech. He criticized with severity the Northern Democracy for its eager and officious subserviency to the South throughout the whole controversy arising out of the Mexican War, hinting that it had been even more eager to server than the South had been to accept its service. He said that the Mexican War had been prosecuted for the purpose of the acquisition of territory for the extension of slavery, but that the nature of the country had defeated, in large part, the hopes of the South. He declared that the whole question of slavery was settled by a higher law than that of Congress and that there was not then a foot of territory whose status was not already fixed by the laws of the several States or the decree of the Almighty; that, by the irrepealable laws of physical geography, slavery was already excluded from California and New Mexico. He "would not take pains uselessly to reaffirm an ordinance of Nature, nor to reenact the will of God." He denounced the Abolitionists and urged upon the Northern States the duty of faithfully and energetically enforcing the abhorred Fugitive Slave Law.

Seward, speaking a few days later, insisted that it was their clear duty to admit California under any Constitution adopted by it, republican in form, and assured then that had its Constitution permitted slavery he would still have deemed it his duty to vote for its admission. He protested against the Fugitive Slave Law as necessarily nugatory and utterly impossible of execution because unanimously condemned by the public sentiment of the North. In answer to the crushing argument that the Constitution carried slavery into the Territories and that cheerful obedience must be yielded to the supreme law, he announced the startling doctrine that there was a HIGHER LAW than the Constitution, to which their first duty was due; that slavery was a violation of this HIGHER LAW and hence the Constitution itself was powerless to establish it in the Territories.

On the 13th and 14th Douglas spoke. The speech was able and adroit. It was marred by the introduction of party-politics into a discussion of such gravity. He was always prone to lapse from statesmanlike dignity to the level of the politician and viewed most matters primarily in their relation to he transient questions of party politics. He undertook the ambitious task of replying to the speeches of Webster, Seward, and Calhoun. He repelled the charge made by Webster that the Northern Democracy had surrendered to the slave power in supporting the annexation of Texas and the Mexican War, declaring that they had supported those measures from patriotic motives, and that he was "one of those Northern Democrats who supported annexation with all the zeal of his nature." "With a touch of the Northwest--the Northwestern Democracy," sneered Webster, who contemptuously looked upon him as a crude blustering youth from the far West. But Webster, whose contempt for his coarse taste was justified, had misjudged his resources and power.

"Yes, sir," replied Douglas, "I am glad to hear the Senator say 'With a touch of the Northwest'; I thank him for the distinction. We have heard so much talk about the North and South, as if those two sections were the only ones necessary to be taken into consideration * * * that I am gratified to find that there are those who appreciate the important truth that there is a power in this Nation, greater than either the North or the South--a growing, increasing, swelling power, that will be able to speak the law to this Nation and to execute the law as spoken. That power is the country known as the great West, the Valley of the Mississippi, one and indivisible from the Gulf to the Great Lakes, stretching on the ones side and the other to the extreme sources of the Ohio and the Missouri--from the Alleghenies to the Rocky Mountains.

"There, sir, is the hope of this Nation, the resting-place of the power that is not only to control but to save the Union. We furnish the water that makes the Mississippi and we intend to follow, navigate and use it until it loses itself in the briny ocean. So with the St. Lawrence. We intend to keep open and enjoy both of these great outlets to the ocean, and all between them we intend to take under our especial protection and keep and preserve as one free, happy, and united people. This is the mission of the great Mississippi Valley, the heart and soul of the Nation and the continent. We know the responsibilities that devolve upon us, and our people will show themselves equal to them. We indulge in no ultraism, no sectional strifes, no crusades against the North and the South. * * * We are prepared to fulfill all our obligations under the Constitution as it is, and determined to maintain and preserve it inviolate in its letter and spirit. Such is the position, the destiny and purpose of the great Northwest."

He told Webster that, according to the doctrine of his 7th of March speech, to permit Texas to be divided into several States would be harmless, because slavery was excluded from a large part of it by the ordinance of Nature, the will of God. He taunted him for not having discovered his now celebrated principle of the ordinance of Nature and will of God until after Taylor's election, and reminded him that prior to the election Cass and Buchanan, the recognized heads of the Democratic party, had advocated leaving the question to the decision of the settlers in the Territories or, in other words, leaving the ordinance of Nature and will of God to manifest themselves. But Webster had then opposed Cass' election and denounced his doctrines and proposed policies. The Whigs, having run counter to the overwhelming popular sentiment in their unpatriotic opposition to the Mexican War, found themselves ruined. They chose a distinguished soldier of that war President, and hoped to rally by adopting this Democratic doctrine.

He accused Seward of carrying New York for the Whigs in the late election by assuring them that Taylor, though a slave-holder, would approve the legislative monstrosity known as the Wilmot proviso, excluding slavery forever from the new Territories. But Taylor had ignored Seward's promise. New York's vote had elected Taylor and a few weeks later Seward was chosen Senator. Taylor was made President and Seward Senator by the latter's successful fraud.

Calhoun's charge of Northern aggression and encroachment he met with a sweeping denial. Neither the North nor the South as such had any right in the Territories, but all the people of the States had equal rights there. The Ordinance of 1787, denounced by Calhoun as a Northern aggression on Southern rights, was voted for by every Southern State. That Ordinance did not, in fact, exclude the South, or even slavery, from the Northwest Territory. A majority of the settlers in Ohio, Indiana and Illinois were from the South. Slavery had actually existed in Indiana and Illinois and had but recently disappeared. The Missouri Compromise was not an act of Northern aggression, but was passed by a united South which had made repeated efforts to extend it to the Pacific. The exclusion of slavery from Oregon was not an act of Northern aggression, but the work of the settlers during the period of joint occupancy under the treaty with Great Britain, and should be accepted by the anti-slavery agitators as proof of the wisdom of popular sovereignty. the objection that the people of the South were forbidden to emigrate with their property to the new Territories was simply a complaint that they could not carry the laws of their States with them, but must be governed by the laws of their new domicile. Calhoun's project of maintaining an equilibrium between free and slave States or of compelling States to accept or retain slavery against their will was impossible.

At the organization of the Government twelve of the thirteen States had slavery. but six of them voluntarily abolished it. Delaware, Maryland, Missouri, Kentucky, North Carolina, and Tennessee would yet adopt the system of gradual emancipation. Seventeen free States would soon be formed out of the territory between the Mississippi and the Pacific. Where would they find slave territory with which to balance these States? If Texas were divided into five States, three of them would be free. If Mexico were annexed, twenty of her twenty-two States would be free by the ordinance of Nature or the will of God. He urged the duty of promptly providing governments for the unorganized domain and closed with a graceful tribute to Clay and the prediction that the Territories would soon be organized, California admitted and the controversy ended forever.

There were three generically distinct groups of statesmen participating in this great debate--the aggressive, unyielding men of the South to whom slavery was dearer than the Union; the temporizing politicians of the North and the border, with their compromises and concessions, hoping to save the Union by salving its wounds; and the stern Puritans of the North, bent on rooting out the sins of the Nation, through the heavens fell.

The climax of the debate was now past, but it continued to agitate Congress until the middle of September. President Taylor, who had exerted his influence against the Compromise, died on July 9th, and was succeeded by Fillmore, who at once called Webster to the head of his Cabinet and turned the Executive influence to the support of the bill. It proved impossible, even with his help, to pass it as a whole; but after it had gone to wreck its fragments were gathered up and each of the several bills which were jumbled together in the "Omnibus" was passed. The great Compromise was accomplished and the slavery question declared settled forever.

Chapter V. Results of the Fugitive Slave Law.

In 1850 Douglas moved to Chicago, which had become the chief city of the State.

The people were greatly exasperated by the passage of the Fugitive Slave Law. The City Council, on October 21st, passed resolutions harshly condemning the Senators and Representatives from the free States who had supported it and "those who basely sneaked away from their seats and thereby evaded the question," classing them with Benedict Arnold and Judas Iscariot. This was a personal challenge to Douglas. It happened that he was absent from the Senate on private business when the bill was passed. But the charge of evading the question was grossly unjust.

On the evening of the 22nd a mass meeting was held at the city hall, attended by a great concourse of angry citizens, who, amid tumultuous applause, resolved to defy "death, the dungeon and the grave" in resisting the hated law. Douglas appeared on the platform and announced that on the following evening he would address the people in defense of the Fugitive Slave Law and the entire Compromise. The announcement was received with a storm of hisses and groans.

The next night an enormous multitude gathered to hear him. The audience was not only sullen but bitterly hostile. After a contemptuous reference to the resolutions and a brief vindication of himself against their insinuations, he plunged into the defense of the law. He insisted that the provision for the return of fugitive slaves contained in the recent act was analogous to the general provision of law for the return of fugitives from justice, and, while abuses of the process might occur and wrong occasionally inflicted, that was one of the inherent infirmities of human law, and the same objection could be urged with equal force to all extradition statutes. While free blacks might be seized in the North and carried South on the false charge of being fugitives from service, innocent white men might also be seized in Chicago and carried to California on the false charge of being fugitives from justice.

He reminded them that the law of 1850 was substantially a reenactment of that of 1793, passed by the Revolutionary Fathers, the founders of the Constitution, and approved by President Washington. He did not argue, but assumed the justice of the old law; nor did he allude to the increased ardor of pursuit of fleeing slaves since their increase in value. He rested his case on the close resemblance of the letter of the new law to that of the old. He told them that the duty of returning fugitive slaves was created not by THIS law, but by the Constitution, and that the real question was not as to the existence of the duty, but which law performed it most justly and efficiently.

A listener asked him whether the Constitution was not in violation of the will of God. He warned them of the danger of that objection, arising from the difficulty of authentically ascertaining the will of God. It was not practicable to allow each citizen to determine it for himself. Hence, certain fundamental principles had been established as a Constitution, which must be assumed to be in harmony with it and from which no appeal lay. The Constitution provided for the return of fugitive slaves. The sacred duty of citizenship bound them to support it. Appeals to a higher law were impracticable and a mere evasion of duty.

Read in a the calmer light of after years the effectiveness of this speech is hard to understand. The literal difference between the recent act and the law of 1793, was not great. But the difference between the ethical views of slavery held by the people in 1850 and those held in 1793 was not to be measured. The changes in the law were vicious and in the opposite direction from the radical changes in popular sentiment. The specially odious provision of the new law, distinguishing it from general extradition statutes, was that forbidding resort to the writ of habeas corpus by the alleged fugitive at the place where seized. The fugitive from justice in California seized in Chicago could, on writ of habeas corpus issued by an Illinois court, have it judicially determined before his deportation whether the facts charged against him constituted a crime and whether thee was probable cause to believe that he had committed it.

Under the new law the Federal Commissioner of the State where the arrest was made had no power to inquire into the truth or sufficiency of the charge. He could only determine whether the person arrested was probably the one who had committed the escape, and must decline to hear the testimony of the fugitive himself. The fact of escape was judicially determined in advance, ex parte, in the State from which it had been made, and the alleged fugitive was remanded to that State for such further proceedings as its laws might provide and "no process issued by any Court, Judge, Magistrate or other person whomsoever" could molest the captor in bearing away his prize.

The speech was adroit, clever and marvelously effective. It strikingly illustrates the mental habits of the times. It sought to stem an irresistible moral current with ingenious plausibilities and appeals to precedent. It treated the question as one of political expediency. It sounded no moral depths, discussed no ethical problem, though the country was aflame with moral indignation and rising passionately against the ethics of the past. It mastered the audience by its fidelity to literal truth and sent them home dazed, troubled, doubtful and ashamed. At the close of the speech resolutions affirming the duty of Congress to pass the Fugitive Slave Law and that of citizens to obey and support it, and repudiating those of the Common Council, were presented and unanimously adopted by the subdued and humbled crowd. On the following night the Council repealed their offensive resolutions.

Meanwhile the country was enjoying the fruits of the Compromise and striving to persuade itself that it would endure. The people earnestly desired to believe that the slavery question was settled forever. So strong was the wish to be done with it that, but for the restless ambition of the politicians, the truce might have been protracted for many years. Permanent peace on the preposterous condition of maintaining on equipoise between active, aggressive and hostile forces was, of course, impossible. but it was confidently expected. Clay, Stephens and fifty-two other Members of the Senate and House issued a manifesto in January, 1851, in which they announced that the Compromise was final and, to give their manifesto the highest solemnity, gravely declared that they would not support anyone for office who was not in favor of faithfully upholding it. In the North approval for the Compromise was general and enthusiastic. It was hoped that money-making would no longer be disturbed by fanatical agitation of moral questions.

And yet there were murmurs of anger against the detested law. It was hard to compel the descendents of the Puritans to hunt down the fleeing slaves when they believed that the curse of God rested on the institution and that the rights of the fugitive were as sacred as those of his pursuers. There were outbreaks of defiance, violent rescues, occasional riots. But resistance was sporadic. The people were disposed to wash their hands of all responsibility for the law, to deprecate its existence, but, since it had been pronounced a final Compromise, to pray that it might prove so. In the South the general opinion was that the danger was past and that years of peace were in prospect. Enthusiastic meetings approving the compromise were held everywhere outside of South Carolina and Mississippi.

While the entire moral victory of the Compromise rested with the people of the South, they had won nothing substantial but the Fugitive Slave Law, which was of questionable value. The great object for which they had conspired, sinned and fought had slipped from their grasp. California was a free State. New Mexico with indecent haste had called a Convention, adopted a Constitution prohibiting slavery, and now demanded admission.

The Compromise, however, bade fair to endure. Fillmore in his annual message in December said, with perfect truth, that a great majority of the people sympathized in its spirit and purpose and were prepared in all respects to sustain it. In Congress an optimistic feeling prevailed. Clay complacently congratulated the country on the general acquiescence in the law and said that it had encountered but little resistance outside of Boston. Douglas assured the Senate that Illinois in good faith discharged its duty under the late Act. It was flanked on the east and west by the slave States of Kentucky and Missouri. It did not intend to become a free negro colony by offering refuge to the fleeing slaves of neighboring States and, not relying on the action of the Federal Government alone for protection, had enacted severe laws of its own to prevent it. When a Judge in that State he had imposed heavy penalties on citizens convicted of the offense of harboring fugitives from service. It was the duty of all citizens to sustain and execute the law, a duty imposed by patriotism and loyalty to the Constitution. But there was an organization in the North to evade and resist the law, with men of talent, genius, energy, daring and desperate purpose at its head. It was a conspiracy against the Government, and men occupying seats in the Senate were responsible for the outrages the Boston mob perpetrated in resistance of the law. The Abolitionists were arming negroes in the free States and inciting them to murder anyone who attempted to seize them under the provisions of the law.

Already he aspired to the Presidency and began to jealously guard his reputation against the sinister suspicions which in those days haunted the ambitious statesman. The great problem which then taxed the ingenuity of the aspiring politician was, how to win the South without alienating the North, or how to hold the North without losing the South. Irreconcilable differences of opinion on fundamental questions, deepening ominously into passionate hostility of sentiment, were already manifesting themselves. The task of the politician was to steer his dangerous course between this Scylla and Charybdis. If he gave color to the suspicion that he even tolerated the growing anti-slavery sentiment of the North, the South would reject him with horror. If he espoused too warmly the cause that had become so dear to the heart of the South, the North, goaded by its over-sensitive conscience, would spurn him with disgust. In the existing state of party organization the highest success was not possible without at least partial reconciliation of these irreconcilable forces. Northern statesmen could not hope to succeed by brave appeals to the passions and prejudices of the South, for they would lose their home constituencies, the worst fatality that can befall an American politician. They could not hope to succeed by brave appeals to the earnest convictions of the North, for they had not yet authority as affirmative rules of political conduct.

The charge of dodging a vote on the Fugitive Slave bill had annoyed Douglas deeply. Any doubt cast upon his fidelity to the South in its contest with the rising anti-slavery sentiment would be disastrous. It was extremely distrustful of Northern politicians and ready to take alarm on the slightest occasion. When the session was but three weeks old he spoke, defending himself against a series of political charges and boasting his partisan virtues in a way that plainly proclaimed the candidate and savored strongly of the stump. He explained that he had been called to New York on urgent private business on the day of the passage of the law and that on his return he was taken seriously ill and confined to his bed during the latter part of the session and for weeks after adjournment. He claimed credit for having written the original Compromise bills which Clay's Committee joined together with a wafer and reported as its own. He denied vehemently having favored the Wilmot Proviso, excluding slavery from all territory acquired from Mexico, and declared that he had sought to extend the Missouri Compromise line to the Pacific. He said that the legislature of Illinois had instructed him to vote for the exclusion of slavery from the Territories, and that, while he had cast the vote of his State according to instructions, he had protested against it, and the vote cast was that of the legislature. He regarded the slavery question as settled forever and had resolved to make no more speeches on it. He assured them that the Democratic party was as good a Union party as he wanted, and protested against new tests of party fidelity and all interpolations of new matter into the old creed. He conjured them to avoid the slavery question, with the intimation that, if they did so, it would disappear from Federal politics forever.

Already the approaching presidential nominations were casting their shadows over the political arena. Though not yet thirty-nine, Douglas was as eager for the Democratic nomination as Webster at seventy was for that of the Whigs.

His picturesque youthfulness, energy and aggressiveness, so strikingly in contrast with the old age, conservatism and timidity of the generation of statesmen with whom he now came in competition, aroused to the highest pitch the enthusiasm of the younger Democrats. It is not impossible that he could have been nominated but for his own imprudence and that of his counselors, who seem to have been more richly endowed with enthusiasm than wisdom. To make sure of getting him before the people in the most dramatic way, and at an early stage, they brought out in the January number of the "Democratic Review" a sensational article which immediately gave him great prominence as a presidential candidate and solidified against him an opposition which assured his defeat.

This famous article said that a new time was at hand, calling for new men, sturdy, clear-headed and honest men. The Republic must have them even if it must seek them in the forests of Virginia or in the illimitable West. It was necessary to have a more progressive Democratic Administration than theretofore. The statesmen of a previous generation, with their antipathies, claims, greatness or inefficiency, must get out of the way. Age was to be honored, but senility was pitiable. Statesmen of the old generation were out of harmony with either the Northern or Southern wing of the party. Those who were not so were men incapable of grasping the difficulties of the times, of fathoming its ideas or controlling its policy. It had been in the power of these superannuated leaders to do much good; but their unfortunate lack of discreet and progressive statesmanship had ruined the party. The next nominee for the Presidency must not be trammeled with ideas belonging to an anterior age, but a statesman who could bring young blood, young ideas and young hearts to the councils of the Republic.

"Your mere general," it continued, "whether he can write on his card the battle-fields of Mexico, or more heroically boast of his prowess in a militia review; your mere lawyer, trained in the quiddities of the court, without a political idea beyond a local election; your mere wire-puller and judicious bottle-holder, who claims preeminence now on the sole ground that he once played second fiddle to better men; * * * and above all, your beaten horse, whether he ran for a previous presidential cup as first or second or nowhere at all on the ticket, none of these will do. The Democratic party expects a new man * * * * of sound Democratic pluck and world-wide ideas to use it on. * * * Let the Baltimore Convention give to this young generation of America a candidate and we are content."

The candidate thus presumptuously demanded by "Young America" was, of course, Douglas. the superannuated statesmen, incapable of grasping difficulties, trammeled by the ideas of an anterior age and sinking into pitiable senility, were clearly, Cass, Buchanan and Marcy. The description of them as the hero of a militia-review, the mere lawyer with his quiddities, the political wire-puller playing second fiddle to better men, was so clear that greater offense could not have resulted from the use of their names.

On June first, 1852, while Congress was still sweltering in the tropical heat of the Capital, the Democratic Convention met at Baltimore, and began its five days of debating and balloting. There was a general belief that the nominee was certain to be elected. The Whigs in their Compromise measures had given the Democrats substantially what they wanted. The chief desire of the latter was to hold fast what they had and secure the administration of the offices. They proposed no reforms, made no complaint against the Administration. Their platform endorsed its chief measure. It pledged the party to the Compromise, including the Fugitive Slave Act, and to "resist all attempts to renew the agitation of the slavery question in congress or out of it, under whatever shape or color the attempt might be made." Like most political platforms, it was made to win votes, not to announce moral truths; and the four statesmen who were competing for the nomination believed that platform best which would offend the fewest prejudices.

The speeches were delivered. the first ballot gave Cass 116, Buchanan 93, Marcy 37 and Douglas 20 votes. Day after day the managers of the three veteran politicians plotted and counter-plotted and "Young America" shouted for Douglas. On the fourth day he had risen to second rank among the candidates, having 91 votes, while Cass had 93. On the fifth day the four distinguished statesmen were dropped and Franklin Pierce, an inoffensive New Hampshire politician, was nominated.

The Whig convention met at Baltimore on June 16th. Already the Whigs, though in power, were demoralized. Their mission, never very glorious, was ended. In the North, tinctured with the old Puritanism and sincere reverence for the primary rights of man, there was a widely diffused feeling that a party responsible for the Fugitive Slave Law could be spared without great loss to civilization.

In the South slavery had definitely placed itself under the protection of the Democratic party as the more reliable, if not the more subservient, of the two. There was an appropriate funereal air about the Convention as it struggled with the question of who should stand on its platform of pitiful negations. The platform solemnly declared that the Compromise Acts, including the Fugitive Slave Law, were acquiesced in by the Whig party as a settlement of the dangerous and exciting questions which they embraced. It insisted upon the strict enforcement of the Compromise and deprecated all further agitation of the question thus settled. If further evidence of the collapse of the party were required, it was furnished by the attitude and character of the candidates. Fillmore was a passive candidate. Webster, his Secretary of State, was an eager competitor. General Scott, though without experience in civil affairs, was the third candidate and received the nomination.

This was the last serious appearance of the Whig party on the stage of national politics. The election resulted in the overwhelming defeat of Scott and the gradual dissolution of the party.

Chapter VI. The Repeal of the Missouri Compromise.

In January, 1853, Mrs. Douglas died. In 1856 he married Miss Adele Cutts of Washington, a Southern lady of good family.

He was reelected Senator in 1853 without serious opposition. He had hitherto been one of the most earnest defenders of the sacredness of the Missouri Compromise. He had strenuously sought to extend it to the Pacific. In 1848 he had declared it as inviolable as the Constitution, "canonized in the hearts of the American people as a sacred thing which no ruthless hand would ever be reckless enough to disturb." But events had moved fast and he moved with them, adjusting his opinions to the advancing demands of the dominant wing of his party.

During half a century the people of the South had been in control of the Government, but Nature and advancing civilization had been steadily against them. They had won a brilliant victory in the Southwest, but found it barren. The only remaining territory in which they could hope to plant slavery was that stretching westward from Missouri, Iowa and Minnesota to the borders of Utah and Oregon. It was wholly unorganized, devoted mainly to Indian reservations. The plan was to organize this region, embracing the present States of Kansas, Nebraska, South Dakota, North Dakota, Montana, and parts of Colorado and Wyoming, into a Territory to be called Nebraska. The final contest between freedom and slavery for the possession of the public domain was now to be waged.

The South was at this time in peculiarly favorable situation. The right to recover runaway slaves was secured. Both the political parties had declared in favor of maintaining and faithfully executing the Compromise. The people of both sections were in favor of maintaining and faithfully executing the Compromise. The people of both sections were in favor of standing by their bargain in good faith, the South enjoying its slavery and the North its freedom in peace. There is no apparent reason why this could not have lasted for many years. But the South could not rest easy under the sense of increasing hostility to slavery and wanted to entrench it more strongly against assault. It would like more Senators and was ready to stake everything on the capture of this last territory out of which new States could be carved.

Congress met for a memorable session on December 5th, 1853. Douglas was chairman of the Committee on Territories, and his trusted lieutenant, Richardson, was chairman of the Territorial Committee of the House. He was thus in position to control the legislation of deepest importance and greatest political interest. During the closing days of the last session Richardson had pushed through the House a bill to organize the Territory of Nebraska. It was reported to the Senate, referred to the Committee on Territories and Douglas attempted in vain to hurry it through.

Dodge of Iowa, now introduced in the Senate a bill for the organization of the Territory which was a copy of the House bill of the last session. It was referred to the Committee on Territories. Douglas as chairman on January 4th reported it to the Senate in an altered form, accompanied by an elaborate report. It provided that when the Territory or any part of it should be admitted as a State it should be with or without slavery as its Constitution should provide. The report justified this non-committal attitude by citing the similar provisions in the Utah and New Mexico bills. It declared it a disputed point whether slavery was prohibited in Nebraska by valid enactment. The constitutional power of Congress to regulate the domestic affairs of the Territories was doubted. The Committee declined to discuss the question which was so fiercely contested in 1850. Congress then refrained from deciding it. The Committee followed that precedent by neither affirming nor repealing the Missouri Compromise, nor expressing any opinion as to its validity. It intimated that in 1850 Congress already doubted its constitutionality. The Compromise was now doomed. The inventive genius of the Senate now applied itself to the task of shifting the odium of its repeal upon the previous Congress.

While this bill was pending in the Senate Douglas was anxiously scanning the field to ascertain what effect it was producing among the people. The South was not likely to be duped. If the Missouri Compromise was in force that alone excluded slavery, and no advantage could accrue from organizing the new Territory without mention of the subject. It did not care to take the risk of proving the law of 1820 invalid. Let it be repealed. But the thought of explicitly repealing the Missouri Compromise, which he had been wont to declare inviolably sacred, appalled him. He dreaded its effect in Illinois and throughout the Puritanical North, where moral ideas were annoyingly obtrusive. The South, though not demanding the repeal of the Compromise, would surely welcome it with joy and gratitude. The question of expediency was a hard one.

The bill, consisting of twenty sections, was printed on January 2d in the Washington Sentinel. Again, on the 10th of January, it appeared in the same paper with another section added. The new section provided that the question of slavery during the territorial period should be left to the inhabitants, that appeals to the Supreme Court should be allowed in all cases involving title to slaves or questions of personal freedom, and that the Fugitive Slave Law should be executed in the Territories as in the States. This remarkable change in the form and spirit of the bill was explained as resulting from an error of the copyist, who had omitted this vital section from it as originally printed.

On the 16th of January Senator Dixon of Kentucky offered an amendment repealing the Missouri Compromise. The next day Sumner gave notice of an amendment affirming it. The question could no longer be dodged. When Dixon's amendment was offered, Douglas, who was greatly annoyed by it, went to his seat and implored him to withdraw it. But he refused. He called upon Dixon and took him for a drive. They talked of the Nebraska bill and the amendment. The result of the conference was that Douglas said to him: "I have become perfectly satisfied that it is my duty as a fair minded national statesman, to cooperate with you as proposed in securing the repeal of the Missouri Compromise restriction. It is due to the South; it is due to the Constitution, heretofore palpably infracted; it is due to that character for consistency which I have heretofore labored to maintain. The repeal will produce much stir and commotion in the free States * * * * for a season. I shall be assailed by demagogues and fanatics there without stint. * * * * Every opprobrious epithet will be applied to me. I shall probably be hung in effigy. * * * * I may become permanently odious among those whose friendship and esteem I have heretofore possessed. This proceeding may end my political career. But, acting under the sense of duty which animates me, I am prepared to make the sacrifice. I will do it."

The bluff Kentuckian was much affected, and with deep emotion exclaimed:

"Sir, I once recognized you as a demagogue, a mere party manager, selfish and intriguing. I now find you a warm hearted and sterling patriot. Go forward in the pathway of duty as you propose, and, though the whole world desert you, I never will."

He had now decided on his course. Cass, who had been forestalled by his alert rival, was understood to be ready to step into the breach if Douglas faltered. He was on perilous heights where a false step would be fatal. Already a storm of opposition was brewing in the North, which would surely break upon him with fury if he proposed the repeal. It might fail in the House and thus leave him with both the North and South angrily condemning him,--the South for his rashness and the North for his treachery. Pierce was known to be opposed to the express repeal of the Compromise. On Sunday, January 22d, Douglas called on the Secretary of War, Jefferson Davis, explained the proposed change and sought the help of the Administration in passing the bill. Davis was overjoyed and at once accompanied him to the White House. Pierce received his distinguished visitors, discussed the plan with them and promised his help.

The next morning Douglas offered in the Senate a substitute for the original Nebraska bill, in which two radical changes appeared. The new bill divided the proposed Territory, calling the southern part Kansas and the northern part Nebraska, and declared the Missouri Compromise superseded by the legislation of 1850 and now inoperative.

On the next day appeared the "Appeal of the Independent Democrats in Congress to the People of the United States." The paper was written by Chase and corrected by Sumner. It denounced the original Kansas-Nebraska bill as a gross violation of a sacred pledge, a criminal betrayal of precious rights, part of an atrocious plot to exclude free labor and convert the Territory into a dreary region of despotism inhabited by masters and slaves, a bold scheme against American liberty, worthy of an accomplished architect of ruin. It declared in a postscript, written after the substitute bill was offered by Douglas on January 23d, that not a man in Congress or out of it, not even Douglas himself, pretended at the time of their passage that the measures of 1850 would repeal the Missouri Compromise. "Will the people," it asked, "permit their dearest interests to be thus made the mere hazards of a presidential game and destroyed by false facts and false inferences?"

The Appeal, which (except the postscript) was written before the substitute was offered, was published in many papers in the North and produced a deep sensation. On the 30th Douglas entered the Senate Chamber angry and excited. He had already begun to hear the distant mutterings of the storm. He opened the debate on his substituted bill, but he was smarting under the cruel lash and, before beginning his argument, poured out his rage on the authors of the Appeal. He accused Chase of treacherously procuring a postponement of the consideration of the bill for a week in order to circulate their libel upon him. Chase interrupted him with angry emphasis. Douglas waxed furious and poured out his "senatorial billingsgate" upon the offenders. Yet, amidst his wrath, he kept his head and made a keen and ingenious defense of his course.

The basis of his argument was the proposition, assumed though no where stated, that while the laws of Congress were specific and enacted to meet particular demands, the PRINCIPLE embodied in each law was general, and if the philosophic principle of any law was repugnant to that of any prior law, however foreign to each other the subjects might be, the latter must be held to repeal the former by implication; that the principle of the legislation of 1850 was repugnant to that of the Missouri Compromise and hence repealed it.

Chase at once replied briefly to the fiery attack, and on February 3d delivered an elaborate speech against the bill, which Douglas recognized as the strongest of the session. As a legal argument it was a complete and crushing answer to the quibbling sophistry of the advocates of implied repeal. But it was not merely the argument of a great lawyer. It was the earnest remonstrance of a moralist who believed in the eternal and immeasurable difference between right and wrong.

He reminded them that the Missouri Compromise was a Southern measure, approved by a Southern President, on the advice of a Southern Cabinet. While in form a law, it had all the moral obligation of a solemn contract. The considerations for the perpetual exclusion of slavery in the Territories north of 36 degrees and 30 minutes were the admission of Missouri with slavery, the permission of slavery in the Territories south of 36 degrees and 30 minutes, and the admission of new States south of that line with slavery if their constitution should so provide. The North had honorably performed its contract by the admission of Missouri and prompt consent to the admission of all other slave States that had sought it. The South had yielded nothing to the North under the contract, except the admission of Iowa and the organization of Minnesota. The slave States, having received all the contemplated benefits under the contract and yielded none, proposed to declare it ended without the consent of the free States. He closed with an appeal to the honor of the South, earnestly imploring the Senators to reject the bill as a violation of the plighted faith and solemn compact which their fathers had made and which they were bound by every sacred obligation faithfully to maintain.

Seward, speaking on the 17th cautioned them that the repeal of the Compromise would be the destruction of the equilibrium between the North and the South so long maintained, the loss of which would be the wreck of the Union. He warned the North that if this territory was surrendered to slavery the South would be vested with permanent control of the Government; for every branch of it would be securely within its power. Already it had absolute sway. One slave-holder in a new Territory, with access to the Executive ear at Washington, exercised more political influence than five hundred free men. The recital of an old repeal was made for the demagogic purpose of confusing the people, but was false in fact and false in law. The Missouri Compromise was a purely local act. That of 1850 was likewise local. They affected entirely different localities. Hence the later law could not by implication repeal the former. It was an ingenious device to attain the desired end by declaring that done by a former Congress which no one then thought of doing, and which the present Congress dared not boldly do. The doctrine of popular sovereignty meant that the Federal Government should abandon its constitutional duty and abdicate its power over he Territory in favor of the first band of squatters who settled within it. It meant that the interested cupidity of the first chance settlers was more fit to guide the destinies of the infant Territory than the collective wisdom of the American people.

Sumner, speaking a week later, declared that they were about to determine forever the character of a new empire. An effort was made on false assumptions of fact, in violation of solemn covenants and the principles of the fathers, to open this immense region to slavery. The measures of 1850 could not by any effort of interpretation, by any wand of power, by an perverse alchemy, be transmuted into a repeal of that prohibition of slavery. The pending proposition was to abolish freedom. When the conscience of mankind was at last aroused, they were about to open a new market to the traffickers in flesh who haunted the shambles of the South. They had as much right to repudiate the purchase of Louisiana as this compact. Despite the temporary success of their political maneuvers, let them not forget that the permanent and irresistible forces were all arrayed against them. The plough, the steam engine, the railroad, the telegraph, the book, were all waging war on slavery. Its opponents could bide the storm of vituperation and calmly await the judgment of the future.

There was at no time the slightest doubt that the bill would pass, and the arguments against it were in the nature of protests against a wrong that could not be averted and appeals to the future to redress it.

From the beginning it had a well organized majority. But, assailed by the invectives of Chase, Seward and Sumner, it could not stand before the world undefended. There was but one man enlisted in its support at all fit to measure swords with any of these great leaders; but he was undoubtedly more than a match for them all.

At midnight on March 3rd Douglas rose to close the debate. The great arguments were delivered; a safe majority was assured. While numerous Senators still wanted to be heard in support of the bill, all conceded his right to close and yielded him the floor. The scenes of that wild night, while he charged upon his foes and stood for hours at bay like a gladiator, repelling their savage assaults, are among the most memorable in our congressional history.

He laughed at the charge that his bill had reopened the slavery question against the will of both political parties, as expressed in their platforms, and had disturbed the country at a time of profound tranquility. These men, he declared, who where singing paeans of praise over the legislation of 1850, were the same men who had most bitterly opposed it and predicted dire results from it, just as they were prophesying evil from the pending measure which simply carried to its legitimate conclusion the beneficent principle of the former law. The substance of all the opposition speeches was contained in their manifesto published in January. Chase in his speech had exhausted the entire argument. The others merely followed in his tracks.

"You have seen them," he said, "on their winding way, meandering the narrow and crooked path in Indian file, each treading close upon the heels of the other, and neither venturing to take a step to the right or left or to occupy one inch of ground which did not bear the footprint of the Abolition champion."

The repeal of the Compromise was a mere incident of the bill. He quoted his speeches in 1850 to show that he then defended the popular sovereignty principle, also resolutions of the Illinois legislature approving it. The Committee assumed in reporting the original bill that the law of 1850 had repealed the Missouri Compromise and hence did not mention it. Finding a diversity of opinion and desiring to clear the ground for the unobstructed operation of the principles of 1850 in all the Territories, they had expressly recited the repeal. Did not the bill as originally reported repeal the Missouri Compromise as effectually as the amended bill did? If so, why this clamor about the amendment? They denounced the original bill in their manifesto as a repeal of the Missouri Compromise. If they told the truth in their manifesto their speeches denouncing the amendment were false. If their speeches were true their manifesto was false. The Missouri Compromise was not a compact at all. It was simply a piece of ordinary legislation, passed like other bills, by means of compromise and concession. The statement that the North had faithfully performed all the terms of he alleged contract and, hence, the South was estopped from repudiating it, was not supported by the evidence. The North had broken it immediately by resisting the admission of Missouri with slavery. A resolution of the New York legislature had been passed a few months after the Compromise instructing their Senators and Representatives to oppose the admission of Missouri or any other State unless its Constitution prohibited slavery. Objection being made to the slavery clause of the Constitution, Missouri had not been admitted until 1821. The North having broken its alleged contract, had relieved the South from all obligation under it, if such obligation ever existed. All this moral indignation had been stirred up over the repeal of an ordinary law. By their manifesto and speeches the anti-slavery Senators had roused the people to rage in their States. The citizens of Ohio had burned him in effigy. He could be found hanging by the neck in all the towns in which they had influence.

Chase protested his sorrow that the people of Ohio had offered this insult. Douglas angrily reminded him of the vituperative epithets contained in the manifesto, which evidently wounded him more deeply than the coarser indignities. He drew Seward and Chase into debate on the literal correctness of details of their arguments, as to which he had the better of them, having fortified himself with voluminous documents, and elaborately proved the inaccuracy of their statements, and elaborately proved the inaccuracy of their statements, which gave him a brilliant opportunity to indulge in a burst of indignation and in his wrath at the errors of his adversaries' neglect, the awkward moral question which, was the core of the controversy. He intimated that Chase and Sumner had obtained their seats in the Senate by questionable compromises. Chase hotly branded the statement as false. Sumner contemptuously denied that he had even sought the position, much less bargained for it. The speech was closed with an earnest appeal to the Senators to banish the subject of slavery forever and refer it to the people to decide for themselves as they did other questions, with assurance that this would result in a satisfactory settlement of the vexed problem and bring abiding peace to all. As the day was dawning he closed.

With difficulty the presiding officer had repressed the bursts of applause in the crowded galleries. Even Seward, moved to admiration by the overwhelming power and marvelous skill of his adversary, impulsively cried out, "I never had so much respect for him as I have to-night."

Amid the solemn hush of anxious expectancy the crowd awaited the calling of the roll. While no one doubted the result, all listened in breathless silence to the voting of the Senators as though it were the voice of doom. Fourteen voted no, and were thirty-seven voted yes. The Senate adjourned amid the loud booming of cannon at the Navy Yard, which celebrated the great victory. In the chill gray dawn, as they stood on the steps of the Capitol and listened to the exultant booming of cannon, Chase said to Sumner:

"They celebrate a present victory, but the echoes they awake will never rest until slavery itself shall die."

The bill now went to the House, where its management was entrusted to Douglas' lieutenant, Richardson, chairman of the Territorial Committee. But the country was aroused. The loud storm appalled the Northern Members, whose votes were needed. Pierce hesitated until goaded on by his Southern counselors. The attempt to refer the bill to the Territorial Committee failed. It was referred to the Committee of the Whole and went to the foot of a long calendar. This alarmed Douglas, who now spent most of his time in the House assisting Richardson. The Administration brought all of its power to bear on the refractory Members, and on the 8th of May the forces were ready for the attack. The House resolved itself into a Committee of the Whole, laid aside all previous business and proceeded to the consideration of the bill. The struggle at once began between the domineering majority and the rebellious minority and continued with increasing bitterness all day, all night and until midnight of the 9th, when the session broke up in angry riot, the enraged members leaping on their desks and shrieking in frenzy or striving to assault each other with deadly weapons.

All were exhausted by the long, sleepless strain, and many were drunk. Douglas was on the floor during most of the session, passing about swiftly among his followers and directing their movements, the master-spirit who guided the storm of his own raising. At midnight the House, now a mere bedlam, adjourned.

The struggle dragged along from day to day, the minority stubbornly contesting every inch, and the majority, under the personal direction of Douglas, hesitating to use their power. At last, on May 22nd, at nearly midnight, the final vote was forced and the bill passed by a majority of thirteen. Among those voting against it was Thomas H. Benton of Missouri, now a Member of the House, after his thirty years' service in the Senate. His terse characterization is more generally remembered than anything else said against it. Speaking with a statesman's contempt of the explanatory clause, he said it was "a little stump speech injected in the belly of the bill."

Chapter VII. The Brewing Storm.

The powerful will and effective energy of the young Senator had achieved a legislative revolution. Perhaps, like Geethe's apprentice, he had called into action powers of mischief which he would not be able to control. With the instincts of the politician he had sought to devise a fundamental principle to meet a passing exigency. He had cooked his breakfast over the volcano.

The whole doctrine of popular sovereignty which became thenceforth the central article in his creed did such violence both to law and philosophy as to discredit the acumen of any statesman who seriously believed it. It was a short lived doctrine, speedily repudiated with disgust by the South, in whose interest it had been invented, and rejected as a legal heresy by a Supreme Court of learned advocates of slavery. It is hardly possible that Douglas believed that Congress could delegate its highest duties and responsibilities to a handful of chance squatters on the frontier. This doctrine, to the establishment of which he devoted a great part of the remaining energies of his life, "meant that Congress, which represented the political wisdom of an educated people, should abdicate its constitutional right of deciding a question which demanded the most sagacious statesmanship in favor of a thousand, or perhaps ten thousand, pioneers, adventurers and fortune seekers, who should happen to locate in the Territory."

The proposition to give the squatters actual sovereignty in all things was an evident reducto ad absurdium. And yet it was the inevitable result of Douglas' reasoning. The only excuse for the existence of territorial governments was that the inhabitants were not yet ready for the duties of self-government. Squatter sovereignty rested on the assumption that there was no such period of immaturity, and hence no period in which territorial governments were justified. The clear logic of the doctrine would entitle the first band of squatters on the public domain to organize a State. But it was a superficially plausible proposition that appealed with peculiar power to the uncritical popular prejudice. The equality of men and the right of self government were the central truths of the American polity. The sentimental devotion to these two principles was passionate and universal. A dogma that seemed to embody them was a rare invention, the supreme feat of the highest order of practical political genius.

But the omens were not good. People seemed absurdly in earnest about this harmless political maneuver. Throughout the North rose a storm of vehement protest, not merely from Abolitionists and Whigs but from insurgent Democrats, which resulted in the consolidation of the incoherent anti-slavery factions into the Republican party and its early conquest of the Democratic States of the Northwest. It developed later that the Northern Democracy was hopelessly ruined by this political masterpiece of the greatest Northern Democrat.

Lincoln, who had been quietly maturing in modest retirement, was roused by this shock and began that memorable battle with Douglas, which finally lifted the obscure lawyer to heights above the great Senator. A resolution endorsing the Nebraska bill was pushed through the Illinois legislature with difficulty, several of the ablest Democrats denouncing it bitterly. Other Northern legislatures either protested against it or remained ominously silent. Throughout the North pulpit and press thundered against the repeal with startling disregard of party affiliations. Three thousand New England clergymen sent a petition protesting against it "in the name of Almighty God." The clergy of New York denounced it. The ministers of Chicago and the Northwest sent to Douglas a remonstrance with a request that he present it, which he did. He was deeply hurt by the angry protests from the moral guides of the people. He denounced the preachers for their ignorant meddling in political affairs, and declared with great warmth that they had desecrated the pulpit and prostituted the sacred desk to the miserable and corrupting influence of party politics. He afterwards said in bitter jest, "on my return home I traveled from Boston to Chicago in the light of fires in which my own effigies were burning."

Congress adjourned early in August, but he lingered in the East and not until late in the month did he return to meet his constituents. The intensity of popular indignation at the North was a disagreeable surprise to him. In Chicago the sentiment was openly and overwhelmingly against him. It was dangerous, now that he had fought his way up to the head of his party and seemed assured of the coveted nomination, to permit himself to be discredited at home.

Four years before he had conquered the hostile city by a speech, and he resolved again to subdue its insurgent spirit. Meetings of disgusted Democrats and indignant Whigs had been held to denounce him. He had been burned in effigy on the streets. He had been charged with loitering in the East afraid to meet the people whom he had betrayed. The changes were rung on the fact that his middle name was that of the traitor, Benedict Arnold. When he entered the city the flags on building and vessels were hanging mournfully at half-mast. At sunset the bells were tolled solemnly. It was truly a funereal reception. Arrangements were made for him to address the people on the night of September 1st in vindication of himself. The meeting was held in the large open space in front of North Market Hall. The crowd was enormous and ominously sullen. The roofs, windows and balconies of all adjacent buildings were occupied. There was not a cheer, except from a little band of friends in front of him, as at nearly eight o'clock he rose to speak.

The memorable scene which followed illustrates how small is the interval that separates the most advanced civilization from the grossest barbarism. He began his speech, but was soon interrupted by a storm of hisses and groans, growing louder and louder until it seemed that the whole enormous throng was pouring out its execration in a mingled hiss and groan. He waited with defiant calmness for the storm to subside and again attempted to speak. He told them with manifest vexation that he had returned home to address his constituents and defend his course and that he intended to be heard. Again he was interrupted by the overwhelming hiss, mingled with groans and coarse insults. His friends fiercely threatened to resent the outrage, but he prudently restrained them. He then began to shout defiance and rebukes at the mob. His combative temper was stirred. He shook his head and brandished his fists at the jeering crowd. His friends importuned him to desist, but he pushed them aside and again and again returned to the attack with stentorian tones and vehement gestures, striving to outvoice the wild tumult and compel an audience.

But they were as resolute as he and persistently drowned his shouting. This continued nearly three hours. At half-past ten, baffled, mortified and angry, he withdrew. One admiring biographer declares that he yelled to the mob as a parting valediction, "Abolitionists of Chicago, it is now Sunday morning. I will go to church while you go to the devil in your own way." The irrepressible conflict was approaching the muscular stage of its development, when the aroused passions of the people must find some other vent than words, when the game of politics could no longer be safely played with the strongest emotions of a deeply moral race.

It was not possible to treat the matter lightly. Evidently a tide of fanatical passion had set against him, not only in the old North, but in the new Northwest, the field of his undisputed mastery. It was necessary to bestir himself in earnest and turn back this rising flood which threatened to engulf him just as he came in sight of his goal. The symptoms were decidedly bad. The elections thus far held indicated a surprising revolt against his new Democratic gospel of popular sovereignty. As the autumn advanced the omens grew worse. New Hampshire and Connecticut had already manifested their disapproval. Iowa, hitherto staunchly Democratic, was carried by the Whigs. The later New England elections showed the most amazing Democratic defection. Pennsylvania elected to Congress twenty-one pronounced opponents of popular sovereignty and slavery extension. Ohio and Indiana had both cast their votes for Pierce. But at this election Ohio rejected the revised Democratic platform by 75,00 and Indiana by 13,000.

After his rebuff in Chicago he plunged into the Illinois campaign, which was fought on the Kansas-Nebraska issue. In the northern part of the State his receptions were chilly and his audiences unfriendly, sometime indulging in boisterous demonstrations of hostility. "Burning effigies, effigies suspended by robes, banners with all the vulgar mottoes and inscriptions that passion and prejudice could suggest, were displayed at various points. Whenever he attempted to speak, the noisy demonstrations which had proved so successful in Chicago were repeated."

But as he moved southward the people became more cordial. The great center of political activity was Springfield, where the State Fair, lasting through the first week of October, attracted thousands of people, and the politicians assembled to make speeches and plan campaigns. He spoke on October 3rd at the State House. The most important matter pending was the choice of the legislature which should elect a Senator to succeed his colleague Shields, who was a candidate for reelection. The opposition was a heterogeneous compound of Whigs, anti-Nebraska Democrats and all other political elements opposed to the revised Democratic creed. The leading candidates of this fusion party for Senator were Lyman Trumbull, a Democrat opposed to the new program of slavery extension, and Abraham Lincoln, the recognized leader of the Whig party of the State. It was expected that Lincoln would answer Douglas on the following day.

This political tourney held in the little Western Capital was in many ways a rather notable event. The great question of human slavery had now definitely passed from the region of mere moral disquisition into that of active statesmanship. It had become the decisive practical problem of the time, the attempt to solve which was revolutionizing party politics and sweeping away the political philosophy of the past. The opinions of men on this question were determining their associations and directing their conduct, regardless of minor matters, which are now forgotten. The South was united for the support and extension of slavery. The North was tending to unity in the resolve to prevent its further spread. Already the new generation of Southern statesmen were plotting to divide the Union and were bent on extending the slave holding States across the continent, believing that when the separation occurred, California would join the Southern Confederation and thus give them a Republic extending from ocean to ocean and controlling the mouth of the Mississippi.

The first step in this plan had already been taken by opening to slavery the Territory of Kansas, which then contained a large part of Colorado. The remaining task of pushing their western border on to the Pacific seemed comparatively easy. Already treason was festering in the heart of the South, but Douglas, now the most powerful ally of these plotting traitors, was entirely devoted to the Union. He neither felt nor thought deeply on any question. The symptoms of coming revolution were merely disclosures of political strategy to him. The South held out the bait of the Presidency, and he led its battle. In his attachment to the Union and his subordination of both morals and statecraft to its preservation as the supreme end, he was a faithful echo of the great statesmen of the preceding age. But a generation of statesmen had appeared in the North with a large and growing following who were reluctantly reaching the conclusion that the primary rights of man were even more sacred than the Union. Political expediency was not their ultimate test of right.

Lincoln, though yet comparatively obscure, was destined soon to become the leader of this new school of ethical statesmen, as distinguished from the old school of political temporizers and opportunists to which Douglas belonged. Lincoln, as Douglas well knew, was a man of finer intellectual gifts than any of the great senatorial triumvirate whom he had successfully met. His moral feelings were tuned to as high a key as Sumner's. He had a firmer grasp of the central truths of the new politico-moral creed than Chase. He had more tact and sagacity than Seward. He had more patience with temporary error, more serene faith in the health and sanity of human nature than any of the three. He was a greater master of the art of popular oratory than any of them. Above all he had the power, dangerous to Douglas, of seizing the most ingenious and artfully concealed sophism and good naturedly dragging it to the light. Endowed with the most exuberant flow of genial humor, he was yet sternly earnest in his belief in the inviolable sanctity of moral right. During his recent years he had read much and thought deeply. He had mastered a style rarely equaled in clearness, simplicity and power. Without the prejudices and entanglements of a past political career, he entered the arena in the ripeness of his slow-maturing powers. Not only his temperament and intellect but his experience and training admirably fitted him for the high task which he was destined to perform.

When Douglas opened his speech at the State House, he unconsciously lent new importance to Lincoln by announcing that he understood that he was to answer him, and requesting him to come forward and arrange terms for the debate. But Lincoln was not present and he plunged into his argument, defending the Kansas-Nebraska bill, his own course and that of his party. Lincoln spoke the next day and among his most eager listeners was Douglas, who occupied a seat in front and was generously invited to reply. The speech, four hours long, was an agreeable surprise to Lincoln's friends, a startling revelation to Douglas and an astonishing event to the crowd, who recognized in the awkward country lawyer a dangerous antagonist for the great Senator, the incomparable master of the art of political debate. He realized that this obscure adversary had clutched him with a power never felt in his great struggles with the giants of the Senate. He indicated his sense of the importance of the contest by devoting two hours to a reply. The chief interest of this meeting now is in the new prominence which it gave to Lincoln. The long duel lasted intermittently through four years, and finally gave Lincoln such fame that he was chose over Seward and Chase to lead the anti-slavery forces which they had roused from lethargy and organized into unity.

The Illinois campaign continued with great spirit and Douglas had the mortification of seeing what he regarded as a wave of fanaticism engulf the State. The anti-Nebraska fusion carried the legislature, defeated Shields and, after a brief contest between Trumball, the anti-Nebraska Democrat, and Lincoln, the anti-slavery Whig, elected the former Senator.

Chapter VIII. Decline of Popular Sovereignty.

Congress had confessed its incompetency to deal with the Kansas problem and referred it to the decision of rude squatters on the frontier. They dealt with this grave congressional question in characteristic fashion. An Emigrant Aid Society, organized in Massachusetts, was among the means adopted by the North to colonize the Territory and mold its institutions. The adventurous frontiersmen of western Missouri were chiefly relied on by the South to shape the new State. The Emigrant Society founded the town of Lawrence and established there a formidable anti-slavery colony. The Missouri squatters organized a "Self-Defensive Association" and attempted to drive out the Northern settlers. Elections were held by the colonists from the North and their Missouri neighbors in which the Missourians outnumbered their rivals and captured the territorial government. The Northern colonists organized a State and attempted to run it. Irregular warfare was maintained between the Lawrence squatters and the invading Missourians to determine which faction was entitled to exercise the sovereignty delegated by Congress.

The House passed a bill to admit Kansas with the Constitution adopted at Topeka by the Northern settlers in their abortive effort to organize a State. It failed in the Senate and a few days later the Federal troops dispersed the usurping State legislature. The Governor seeing that all civil authority was ended, negotiate a truce between the warring factions, resigned and hastened away from the scene of the disastrous experiment of Squatter Sovereignty.

The meeting of Congress on December 3rd, 1855, marked another stage in the great struggle. So completely were the parties disorganized that it was found impossible to classify this Congress. From December 3rd to February 2nd the House was unable even to organize itself. On December 31st the President sent in his message. He disposed of the overshadowing problem in a few brief words and devoted the message to ephemeral matters long since as completely forgotten as himself. Although civil war had been raging in Kansas for many months and the carnival of crime was still in progress on that frontier, he gravely assured Congress that it was a matter of congratulation that the Republic was tranquilly advancing in a career of prosperity and peace. He told them that the people of the Territory were clothed with the power of self-government and that he had not felt justified in interfering with their exercise of that right. But on January 24th he sent another message announcing in general terms the disappointment of his hopes and recommending an enabling act for the admission of Kansas as a State.

The Senate consisted of thirty-four Democrats, twelve Whigs and thirteen Republicans. Douglas was the recognized leader of the majority, without whose presence they were unwilling to take any decisive action. But he was detained by sickness and did not take his seat until February 11th.

On the 12th of March he presented to the Senate a most elaborate report from his Committee, together with a bill to authorize the people of Kansas to organize a State whenever they should number 93,420.

It is impossible to read this report, which was prepared by himself, without admiring his subtle art and consummate skill. He argued away the power of Congress to impose restrictions on new States applying for their admission, other than that the Constitution be republican in form, and insisted that the people of the Territories must be left perfectly free to form their own institutions and were entitled to admission as matter of right. He traced the trouble to the pernicious activity of the Emigrant Aid Company, which had attempted to force New England institutions and customs upon the Territory. He accused this Company of systematic colonization and drew a moving picture of the march of these political colonists across Missouri, pouring out their denunciations of slavery, exhibiting their hostility to the institutions of that State, until at last the people in alarm resolved on defense. He admitted that there might be some cause for regret over the occasional errors and excesses of the Missourians; but it must not be forgotten that they were defending their internal prosperity and domestic security against the invasion of New England fanatics, who were bringing in their grain "the horrors of servile insurrection and intestine war."

The attempt to organize a State government at Topeka he condemned as a seditious movement, designed to overthrow the territorial government and the authority of the United States. He justified the law referring the question of slavery to the inhabitants, and traced its failure to the intemperate passions of those who had precipitated this mad contest for mastery.

Collamer of Vermont presented the minority report, condemning the violence of the friends of slavery, deploring the fearful results of the experiment of Squatter Sovereignty and urging speedy admission of the State. It condemned the provision of the law referring the question of slavery to the inhabitants and traced the entire trouble to that blunder.

Sumner at once denounced the report of the majority, intimated his purpose of properly setting the brand of falsehood upon it in a subsequent speech, and told them to "begin their game with loaded dice."

Douglas angrily challenged him to deny a single fact in the report and said he was ready to overwhelm him with proof. "We are ready to meet the issue," he said, "and there will be no dodging. We intend to meet it boldly; to require submission to the laws and to the constituted authorities; to reduce to subjection those who resist them, and to punish rebellion and treason. I am glad that a defiant spirit is exhibited here; we accept the issue."

Two days later Trumbull spoke in unsparing criticism of the report of the Committee. It happened that Douglas was absent when he began. Word was carried to him and he hurried to the Senate. When Trumbull closed and the usual motion to adjourn was made, he protested against it and denounced the discourtesy of discussing the report during his absence. He was vexed especially by his colleague's exasperating statement that was a "life-long Democrat and was representing the Democracy of Illinois in the Senate." He assured them that Trumbull was without party standing in that state, and proposed that they sign a joint resignation, thus submitting their quarrel to the people. But there was a deeper wound than this which still rankled, and he turned from his colleague to pour out his wrath on Sumner for the publication of the "Appeal of the Independent Democrats," and the old quarrel between them was rehearsed anew with increasing bitterness on both sides.

On the 20th he spoke for two hours and a half in defense of his report. Charges of fraud, violence or illegal voting, he said, were made in but seven of the eighteen election districts into which Kansas was divided, although ample provisions had been made for the presentation of protests to the Governor. A large majority of both branches of the legislature were elected by these eleven districts where no complaints were made. At least a quorum must have been legally elected. The minority report charged that on the day of the territorial election, "large bodies of armed men from the State of Missouri appeared at the polls in most of the districts, and by most violent and tumultuous carriage and demeanor, over-awed the defenseless inhabitants and by their own votes, elected a large majority of the members of both houses of said Assembly."

But the report contained not a word about the eleven uncontested districts affected by this invasion. In the eleven uncontested districts the judges made their returns in due form and, no protests nor charges of fraud or illegal voting being presented, the Governor granted certificates of election as a matter of course. The minority stated that in many districts protest had not been made because the inhabitants, discouraged and intimidated by the Missouri invaders, had let the matter pass. Yet at Lawrence and Leavenworth, the chief centers of the alleged Missouri violence the people were not intimidated from contesting the election, what reason was there to suppose that elsewhere, remote from the scene of trouble, they were so completely conquered that they dared not protest against their wrongs and petition for redress of their grievances?

The thirty-three judges appointed by the Government to conduct the election in the eleven districts, all swore that the returns contained a true statement of the votes polled by the lawful voters. The Governor, two weeks after giving certificates of election, issued his proclamation commanding the members to assemble on the 2d of July. He recognized the legitimacy of the legislature in his message, invoking the Divine blessing on it and recommending the passage of important laws. But he afterward quarreled with the legislature. He then sought to repudiate it and impeach its validity by charging that it had been elected by Missouri invaders. The only evidence before the Committee tending to show irregularities in the election was the hearsay statement of the Governor, which flatly contradicted his solemn official declarations. The legislature itself had investigated the elections of all members against whom contests were filed and its legitimacy was finally and conclusively established. The malcontents having failed to capture the legislature, encouraged by Governor Reeder (who had meanwhile been relieved from office), instituted their rebellious Topeka movement and, in defiance of the law, attempted to organize a State.

The movement was revolutionary and intended to subvert the existing Government. Only two laws enacted by the territorial legislature were complained of as unjust,--that relating to elections and that relating to slaves. The social, domestic and pecuniary relations of the people had adjusted themselves to this body of laws which Congress was asked to annul; and these friends of the negro who had organized a rebellious State government in his behalf, had adopted a Constitution which forever excluded him from the State. The entire trouble in Kansas, he continued, rose not from any vice inherent in the law, but from abuses of the rights given by it to the people. The law simply permitted them to form their domestic institutions in their own way. If that great principle had been permitted free operation, there would have been no violence or trouble in Kansas. The good order reigning in Nebraska, where the law was fairly tried, was sufficient proof of its wisdom.

The opponents of this great principle had insisted on moulding the State of Kansas from without. Having failed to induce Congress to interfere in the internal affairs of the Territory, they then sought to accomplish their purpose by means of a society organized in Washington and charted in Massachusetts, with several millions of capital. They had deliberately attempted to discredit the Kansas-Nebraska bill and its supporters, in order to influence the approaching presidential election. The whole responsibility for the disturbance in Kansas rested upon the Massachusetts Emigrant Aid Company and its affiliated societies. The people of Missouri never contemplated the invasion of conquest of the Territory. If they had imitated the example set by New England, they had done it on the principle of self-defense, and had always been ready to abandon their counter-movement as soon as the managers of the New England invasion ceased their efforts to shape the domestic institutions of the Territory by an unwarranted scheme of foreign interference. When the cardinal principle of self-government should be recognized as binding on all, there would be an end of the slavery controversy, and the occupation of political agitators, whose hopes of position and promotion depended upon their capacity to disturb the country, would be gone.

The debate lingered along indecisively through the Spring weeks and the Senators poured out their mutual recriminations with increasing bitterness. Personal relations among them were seriously strained. Both parties were conscious that their constituents shared their passions and applauded their acrimony.

On the 19th and 20th of May, Sumner delivered his philippic on "The Crime Against Kansas." The title of the speech was a gratuitous insult to the power which had held sway in American politics for fifty years and learned to enjoy that sense of superiority and sacredness which characterized the hierarchy in the middle ages. The assaults on brother Senators were brutal. Senator Butler of South Carolina, a polite, formal gentleman of the old school, was recognized as the social and intellectual head of the Southern aristocracy. Douglas, though forever excluded from its inner circles, was an efficient and useful ally.

These senatorial leaders of the slavery crusade in Kansas were the victims of Sumner's bitter invective. He referred to them as the Don Quixote and Sancho Panza of slavery and, as if to prove that this comparison was not a mere momentary inspiration of playful humor but the elaboration of malignant hate, he developed the parallel to its minute details. He described Douglas in his speech defending his report as "piling one mass of elaborate error on another mass and constraining himself to unfamiliar decencies of speech." But he drew hope from the reflection that the Illinois Senator "is but mortal man; against him is immortal principle. With finite power he wrestles with the Infinite and he must fall. Against him are stronger battalions than any marshaled by mortal arm, the inborn, ineradicable, invincible sentiments of the human heart; against him is Nature with all her subtle forces; against him is God. Let him try to subdue these." He compared the Kansas troubles to the barbarous warfare of the Scottish Highlands when blackmail was levied and robberies committed by marauders "acting under the inspiration of the Douglas of other days," and compared Douglas' recent speech to "the efforts of a distinguished logician to prove that Napoleon Bonaparte never existed."

Douglas answered with extreme bitterness. He declared that Sumner's speech had been got up like a Yankee bedquilt by sewing all the old scraps and patches together. He pronounced his classic quotations obscene and indecent.

"Is it his object," he asked, "to provoke some of us to kick him as we would a dog in the street? * * * * * The Senator from Massachusetts," he declared, "had his speech written, printed, committed to memory, and practiced every night before the glass, with a negro boy to hold the candle and watch the gestures." He charged Sumner with perjury in taking the senatorial oath to his personal grievance and complained that he had been burned and hung in effigy under the advice of Sumner and his brother agitators because of his unswerving devotion to the Constitution.

"I wish," he said, "the Senate to bear in mind that in the many controversies in which I have been engaged since I have been a member of this body, I never had one in which I was not first assailed. I have always stood on the defensive. You arrange it on the opposite side of the house to set your hounds after me and then complain when I cuff them over the head and send them back yelping. I never made an attack on any Senator; I have only repelled attacks." He warned Sumner that Butler, who was absent during the speech, would return to speak and act for himself.

Sumner briefly replied, defending himself against the charge of disloyalty to the Constitution in his unwillingness to support its fugitive slave clause, by quoting Jackson's famous dictum that each man swears to support the Constitution as he understands it. He then turned on Douglas with bitter scorn. He rebuked him for his coarse personalities unbecoming a Senator and a gentleman.

"Let him remember," he said, "that the bowie-knife and bludgeon are not the proper emblems of senatorial debate. Let him remember that the swagger of Bob Acres and the ferocity of the Malay cannot add dignity to this body. * * * * I will not go into the details which have flowed out so naturally from his tongue. I only brand them to his face as false. I say also to that Senator, and I wish him to bear it in mind, that no person with the upright form of man can be allowed--" He hesitated in doubt whether to proceed.

"Say it," exclaimed Douglas.

"I will say it," replied Sumner. "No person with the upright form of man can be allowed, without violation of all decency, to switch out from his tongue the perpetual stench of offensive personality. Sir, that is not a proper weapon of debate, at least on this floor. The noisome, squat and nameless animal to which I now refer is not a proper model for an American Senator. Will the Senator from Illinois take notice?"

"I will," answered Douglas, "and therefore will not imitate you in that capacity, recognizing the force of the illustration."

"Again," replied Sumner, "the Senator has switched his tongue and again he fills the Senate with its offensive odor."

Two days after the speech, Preston H. Brooks, a relative of Butler, who represented a district of South Carolina in the House, entered the Senate Chamber after adjournment and, finding Sumner in his seat writing, approached him and struck him down with a heavy cane. There was a brief struggle in which Sumner was stunned and severely injured.

When the assault occurred Douglas was in the reception room adjoining the Senate Chamber conversing with friends. A messenger ran in shouting that someone was beating Mr. Sumner. He rose intending to interfere in the fray, but, recalling their unpleasant relations, returned to his seat. When the violence was ended he went to the Chamber to see the result. Sumner, dazed, bruised and bleeding, had been helped to his feet and was leaning against a chair. Douglas cast a momentary glance at the victim of this brutal and cowardly outrage, then passed on without comment.

On the day before the assault, the Missouri ruffians had sacked the town of Lawrence. On the day following, John Brown's Pottawotamie adventure occurred. A crisis was at hand imperiously demanding more effective action on the part of Congress. The country was aroused, alarmed and horrified. The Conventions were to be held in June and it was necessary that the Democrats bestir themselves and make some disposition of the harassing problem of Kansas. The existing condition in the hag-ridden Territory was directly chargeable to a measure whose authorship Douglas had boasted. There was danger that the tragic failure of his masterpiece of state-craft would wreck his party and load his own name with odium which even his rugged vitality could not throw off. Such uncontrollable passion had been stirred by his pending bill that it seemed prudent to quietly drop it.

On the 24th of June, Toombs introduced a bill providing for the taking of a census, the holding of an election of delegates to a Constitutional Convention, and the orderly organization of a State. It was referred to Douglas' Committee, which promptly reported back an amended bill so infinitely better than the measures thus far attempted that it seemed comparatively just. It provided for the appointment of commissioners to prepare lists of all citizens over twenty-one years old resident in the Territory since the 4th of July, who were to vote at the election; also for the holding of a Convention, the drafting of a Constitution and the admission of the State.

There were three objections to the bill. The commissioners were to be appointed by President Pierce. The 4th of July, from which residence must date, was a time at which great numbers of Northern settlers would be absent from the Territory on account of the turbulence and disorder which had rendered life there not only uncomfortable but unsafe. Moreover, no express provision was made for submitting the Constitution to a vote. However, it was regarded as a concession to the demands of an aroused public, clothed with the power of promptly and authoritatively expressing its disapproval.

But there were those in the Senate who feared the gift-bearing Greeks and thought it well, now that the majority had shown some regard for public opinion, to insist upon an explicit declaration of their purpose to submit the slavery question to the people of the Territory fairly and without juggling tricks. On the 2d of July, Trumbull offered an amendment declaring it to be the true intent and meaning of the bill organizing the Territory of Kansas to confer upon the inhabitants "full power at any time, through its territorial legislature, to exclude slavery from said Territory or to recognize and regulate it therein."

This amendment seemed with utmost fairness to declare the meaning of that law precisely as Douglas expounded it. But the South had already taken the advanced ground that, as the Constitution of the United States expressly established slavery, it was not within the power of Congress or its creature, the territorial legislature, to abolish it. This was not the creed of the Northern Democracy, which had embraced the popular sovereignty doctrine of Douglas and Cass. To abandon that doctrine was to alienate the Northern Democrats and lose the presidential election. To carry it out in good faith was to surrender Kansas and the remaining Territories to anti-slavery institutions; for it was already evident that popular sovereignty meant free States. It was at no time a part of the serious political philosophy of the South, but the ingenious invention of the Northern leaders to hold their following. The South had permitted is Northern allies to give currency to the doctrine, but the more sagacious saw that it was a failure and were preparing, when the election was over, to cast it aside and announce the true Southern dogma, that no sovereignty except that of a State could forbid slavery anywhere in the Union.

Already the Dred Scott case was pending in the Supreme Court and had been once argued; but the decision was reserved until the elections were over and the new President inaugurated. Well informed Southern statesmen did not doubt that this ultra doctrine of their party would receive the authoritative sanction of that tribunal and the temporary scaffolding of popular sovereignty would then be summarily kicked aside. They could not afford to adopt Trumbull's declaration of power in the Territory to abolish slavery, for they secretly expected to establish that it had no such power. They could not afford to frankly declare against it while still courting the Northern Democrats. Benjamin, who was an accomplished lawyer, and with the lawyer's instincts depended more on constitutional defenses than on wavering popular majorities, moved to add the words "subject only to the Constitution of the United States." Now that the Constitution had become the bulwark of slavery, there was nervous dread that Congress and the people might forget that it was the supreme law to which all legislation was subject. Douglas earnestly objected to Trumbull's amendment. He protested against it as wholly unnecessary. He also voted against it as did the great majority of the Senators.

The bill passed the Senate by a vote of 33 to 12; but the House declined to consider it, and on the 3d passed an act to admit Kansas under the Topeka Constitution. No compromise of differences so radical was possible. Douglas remarked truly to his biographer that "it was evident during all the proceedings that the Republicans were as anxious to keep the Kansas question open as the Democrats were to close it, in view of the approaching presidential election."

Chapter IX. The Conventions of 1856.

Douglas was now at the zenith of his success, master of all his resources, the most admired, dreaded and powerful man in American public life. History must inexorably condemn much of his most brilliant and successful work, but the very emphasis of its condemnation is an involuntary tribute to the matchless efficiency of the man. At this period he was the most masterful and commanding personage of purely civil character that has "strutted his hour upon the stage" of American politics. The cabinet maker's apprentice, the village schoolmaster, the Western lawyer, had, by sheer force, established his right to this position of real master of his country. A weak President was cringing at his feet. He had overcome the brilliant and powerful opposition in the Senate. The aristocratic South, which instinctively dreaded and despised a plebeian, was paying him temporary homage.

He was barely 43 years old. So strenuous and effective had been his youth that people hesitated to set bounds to his future possibilities. So strongly had his overmastering force impressed the popular imagination that the sobriquet, "Little Giant," suggested by his small stature and enormous energy, had become household words. He had come to Washington fifteen years before, a crude, coarse, blustering youth, as described by the accomplished Adams whose social ideals were borrowed from the courts of Europe. But he had readily adjusted himself to his new environment and taken on the polish of the Capital. Though never rich, he made money with ease and spent it with princely munificence. He was not only the political dictator but the social lion of Washington. He lived in splendid style, in harmony with his exalted station, entertained generously and responded freely to the numerous invitations of friends and admirers. "His ready wit, his fine memory, made him a favorite. * * * * He delighted in pleasant company. Unused to what is called etiquette, he soon adapted himself to its rules and took rank in the dazzling society of the Capital. * * * To see him threading the glittering crowds with a pleasant smile or kind word for everybody one would have taken him for a trained courtier."

Tradition, backed by General McClellan, says he was a heavy drinker, though not a drunkard, and some of his finest speeches at this period of his life appear to have been delivered after unrestrained carousals that would have prostrated ordinary men.

Ever since 1852, when his youth and indiscretion had defeated his presidential aspirations, he had been waiting impatiently for the Convention of 1856. During the past four years he had been conspicuously "riding in the whirlwind and directing the storm" of politics. He had perhaps intensified the hostile prejudices of the New England Puritans; but they were austere moralists, rather than progressive politicians. He had certainly alienated many friends in the Northwest, which was slowly withdrawing from its old alliance with the South, and falling into sympathy with the stern and uncompromising East. But, while he regretted the necessity of giving offense to any section of the country or any body of the people, he had deliberately chosen what he deemed the less of two political evils,--the alienation of the Puritans of New England and the Northwest rather than a breach with the salve holding baronage of the South, which had established a prescriptive right to control the Presidency. And yet the fact could not be blinked that all his services and sacrifices to the South had failed to give him its confidence and the enthusiastic loyalty that springs from it. It viewed him with mingled emotions of admiration and fear. It desired to retain his service but was unwilling to trust him with power. It could not forget that in his zeal for its service that he had trifled with the North and suspected that, if self-interest prompted, he might break faith with the section which he now served with such ardor.

The South, a decided minority in population, had long held its sway by artful appeals to the selfish ambition of Northern politicians. Although the undisputed command of the Democracy was in its hands and the burning question of the time was that of slavery, no Southern man had in late years been permitted to enter the field as a candidate for the Presidency. The Southern leaders inexorably insisted on giving the nomination to Northern men. There were at this time three candidates from the North; Pierce, how would have joyfully submitted to any terms and pledged himself to any service for another four years of office; Buchanan, the great lawyer and distinguished statesman, who had just returned from the English mission; and Douglas, the giant of the Senate, the recognized head and practical dictator of his party.

In point of ability and energy there was no comparison between Douglas and either of his competitors. Pierce had laboriously earned for himself the lasting contempt of the world. Buchanan was an eminently respectable, dignified old gentleman of great professional attainments and diplomatic experience, an admirable Ambassador, a good Secretary of State, who might even have adorned the Supreme Bench, but whose vacillating will and temporizing character hopelessly unfitted him for the arduous duties of the Presidency in the great crises that ensued. Had the positive, combative and masterful Douglas been nominated at this time it may be safely said that the most momentous chapter of American history would have been widely different from what it is.

The Convention met at Cincinnati on the 2d of June and continued in session for five days. The platform was adopted without dissent, declaring the firm purpose of the party to "resist all attempts at renewing, in Congress or out of it, the agitation of the slavery question," and "recognizing and adopting the principle contained in the organic law establishing the Territories of Nebraska and Kansas as embodying the only sound and safe solution of the slavery question."

Buchanan's candidacy was engineered with rare skill. He was fortunate in having been absent from the country, representing his Government at the Court of St. James, during the three preceding years crowded with great and stirring events, while Pierce and Douglas had been skirmishing for the advantage, each seeking to outbid the other in eager competition for Southern favor. The South was deeply indebted to Douglas; but fear is strong than gratitude. It was well satisfied with Pierce, but hesitated to nominate him lest he might be overwhelmed with a storm of just contempt. Without an element of positive strength, Buchanan was a formidable candidate. On the first ballot he had 135 votes, Pierce 122, Douglas 33, and Cass 5. Pierce lost steadily for 14 ballots while Buchanan and Douglas gained. Pierce's name was then withdrawn. On the next ballot Buchanan had 168 and Douglas 118 votes. Douglas then sent a dispatch to Richardson, his manager, to withdraw his name and make the nomination of Buchanan unanimous.

On June 17th the first Republican National Convention was held at Philadelphia. It was not yet a united and well organized party. It made little pretense of agreeing in anything but unyielding opposition to slavery-propagandism and the fixed resolve to curb the intolerable arrogance of the slave power. It was made up of those who were opposed to the repeal of the Missouri Compromise, to the further extension of slavery, and to the refusal to admit Kansas as a free State. It consisted of Whigs, Free-spoilers, Know-nothings and Democrats, who were inclined to apologize for their temporary association under the name of this mushroom upstart and were not willing to have it forgotten that their essential political creeds were unchanged. They were Republicans for a time until their own parties reformed or gathered strength for more effective work.

Yet, imperfect as was the organic unity of the party, it contained a large part of the best political ability of the country. The real leaders, who had evolved it from the incoherent chaos of earlier years, impressed their energetic characters upon the organization, and prescribed for it such formula of faith as it yet had, were Seward and Chase. To one of them the nomination was clearly due. Seward preferred to wait four years. It was not deemed prudent to nominate Chase. On the first formal ballot John C. Fremont was nominated. For the office of Vice-President Abraham Lincoln received 110 votes, but was fortunately defeated. The platform declared it to be "the right and duty of Congress to prohibit in the Territories those twin relics of barbarism, polygamy and slavery," condemned in scathing terms the conduct of affairs in Kansas and demanded its immediate admission under the Topeka Constitution.

An exciting campaign followed. Rallies, parades, fireworks and theatrical displays were lavishly provided by the sanguine Republicans. Their orators filled the land with eloquent denunciation of the Pierce Administration and the Buchanan platform. Much as it outwardly resembled the log cabin and hard cider campaign of 1840, it was wholly different in character. The Republicans were in serious earnest. They had well defined, though discordant opinions and convictions. But before the end of the contest it was clear that they had blundered in nominating the picturesque "pathfinder."

Douglas was not inactive during the campaign, being deeply interested, not only in the election of Buchanan, but in restoring Democratic supremacy in Illinois.

He sold a hundred acres of land on the western limit of Chicago for a hundred thousand dollars and contributed with great liberality to the campaign fund, not only of his own State, but also of Pennsylvania. The Democrats won both States, which, with the entire vote of the South, elected Buchanan.

Millard Fillmore, a rather ghostly reminiscence of other days, had been nominated by the American and Whig parties and carried Maryland. The combined vote of Fremont and Fillmore exceeded that of Buchanan by nearly half a million. The Democrats were evidently approaching a crisis, and harmony, never so imperatively needed as now, was never so hopelessly unattainable.

Chapter X. Popular Sovereignty in the Supreme Court.

The anger of the world was rising against American slavery. It was confessedly a shocking anomaly in our system of universal freedom and democratic equality. The people of the slave States were inflexibly resolved to maintain and extend it in defiance of the rising sentiment of the age. For many years they had succeeded in holding their ground and stifling the anti-slavery agitation. They had vigilantly kept control of the Government. During sixty of the first sixty-eight years the presidential chair had been occupied by Southern men or their dependents. The Senate had uniformly, and the House usually, been under their sway. The Supreme Court had also been composed of Southern men. Now that slavery was forced to fight for its life, the South with increased energy sought the active support of all the departments of Government. Pierce was its humble servant. The efficient and imperious Douglas was serving it in the Senate, and Cass was an eager rival. The Northern Democracy followed their lead. A majority of the Supreme Court were zealous advocates of slavery. It was unfortunate for the South, and for Douglas, that the champions of Southern rights on the bench and their advocates in Congress could not have understood each other in advance. They were seeking to plant slavery on a safe foundation and gird it round with impregnable defenses. Douglas had promulgated the doctrine of squatter sovereignty with which the South was not satisfied. It was possible for the Court to devise a safer remedy for the threatened dangers.

In 1834, there was an army surgeon named Dr. Emmerson living in Missouri who owned a slave named Dred Scott. He was transferred to Fort Snelling in the Territory of Wisconsin and took his slave with him, but in 1838 he returned with him to his former home. He then sold Scott to a man named Sanford, who resided in New York, but kept his slaves in Missouri. In 1854 the slave brought an action in the United States Circuit Court of Missouri to recover his freedom, on the ground that he had been voluntarily taken into the Territory of Wisconsin, where, by the act of Congress known as the Missouri Compromise, slavery was prohibited. His case rested upon the rule that slavery, being the creature of positive municipal law, had no legal existence beyond the limits of the sovereignty creating or recognizing it. The law of Missouri establishing slavery was of no efficacy in Wisconsin. Hence, it was urged, when Dred was taken to that Territory, the relation of master and slave ended and he became a free man.

Upon its merit the case presented but one question: Was slavery forbidden in Wisconsin? There rose, however, a preliminary question of great importance. To give the Federal Court jurisdiction it was necessary to show that the plaintiff and defendant were citizens of different States. Scott alleged that he was a citizen of Missouri and Sanford a citizen of New York. The answer denied the jurisdiction of the Court for the reason that Scott was not a citizen of any State, being a negro slave, and hence not entitled to maintain his action. The Circuit Court overruled this plea, but held Scott to be still a slave, notwithstanding his sojourn in Wisconsin, and awarded him to Sandford. The case was taken to the Supreme Court and there argued by lawyers of great ability and learning. The Court found unusual difficulties in it, held it under advisement during the exciting summer of 1856, and directed a re-argument at the December term. On March 6th, 1857, two days after the inauguration of Buchanan, the Judges delivered their memorable opinions.

At this time the Court consisted of five Southern Democrats, two Northern Democrats, one Whig and one Republican. Chief Justice Taney wrote the opinion of the Court, and did it in a manner likely to preserve his name from early oblivion. Judges McLean and Curtis filed dissenting opinions.

The Court, after holding that Scott could not maintain his action for want of citizenship, decided among other things that: "Whatever the General Government acquires it acquires for the benefit of the people of the several States who created it. It is their trustee, acting for them and charged with the duty of promoting the interests of the whole people of the Union. * * * * The right of property in a slave is distinctly and expressly affirmed in the Constitution. The right to traffic in it, like an ordinary article of merchandise and property, is guaranteed to the citizens of the

United States. * * * * The Government * * * is pledged to protect it in all future time. * * * * The act of Congress which prohibits a citizen from holding and owning property of this kind in the territory of the United States north of the line mentioned (36 degrees 30 minutes) is not warranted by the Constitution and is therefore void. * * * * * If Congress cannot do this it will be admitted that it could not authorize a territorial legislature to do it."

Thousands of copies of the opinion of Judge Taney were printed and distributed among the people by the Democrats who, at first, were so elated over the blow dealt to the Republican fanatics that they overlooked the fact that the decision was even more fatal to the favorite doctrine of the Northern wing of their own party.

The dissenting opinions were printed in enormous numbers by Republican committees and distributed among the anti-slavery people of the Northern and Middle States. Far from settling the controversy, the powerful conflicting opinions confirmed the already inveterate prejudices and disclosed with scientific clearness the fact, long dimly felt, that there existed two fundamentally different and irreconcilably hostile theories of government among the people which must sooner or later grapple for the mastery. Naturally among Northern Democrats the first emotion on hearing of the decision was exultation over the disastrous reverse suffered by the Republicans, whose whole political creed seemed annihilated. They had declared in sounding phrase that it was the duty of Congress to wipe from the Territories those twin relics of barbarism, slavery and polygamy; and promptly the Supreme Court had decided that Congress had no such power. But it soon grew uncomfortably clear to them that while the decision upset the favorite dogma of the Republicans, it was utterly inconsistent with the doctrine of popular sovereignty, the fundamental tenet of Northern Democratic faith. The decision was not only a victory of the Democrats over the Republicans, but a complete victory of the Southern slave-holding Democracy over that of the free North.

To Douglas the situation in which this left his party was disastrous. Restlessly active and efficient as he had been in the practical management of political affairs, his distinctive achievement had been the powerful advocacy of the doctrine of popular sovereignty, of which, if not the original author, he was at least the chief sponsor. With this doctrine his fame as a statesman was indissolubly linked. On its success the unity of the Northern wing of his party depended; on which hung his hopes of victory.

Two days before the opinion was announced President Buchanan in his inaugural address reminded the people that the great question which had agitated them so long would soon be settled by the Supreme court and bespoke general acquiescence in its decision. This unhappy allusion gave rise to the unpleasant suspicion that the relation between the new President and the Supreme Court in their common service of the South was unduly intimate.

Had Douglas been great enough to sink the politician in the statesman, he would now have broken with the Southern wing of his party, which had contemptuously repudiated his entire system of political doctrines; he would have rejected the new dogma imposed upon his party by the Southern dictators and led the assault upon this new creed, which was not only fatal to himself as a National statesman, but could not fail ultimately to prove fatal to his party and involve his country in the horrors of civil war. His squatter sovereignty was pitiful enough. But this new doctrine, announced by the Supreme Court, and approved by the President and his party, stripped the settlers in the Territories of all semblance of sovereignty and planted slavery among them by the self-acting energy of the Constitution, in utter disregard of their wishes. On the most important question then pending his party had reached a conclusion which he believed to be utterly wrong. But it was his opinion that moral ideas had no place in politics. He could not break with the powerful party which he had led so long. He could not unqualifiedly endorse the new doctrine without stultifying himself. He attempted the impossible task of reconciling the new creed with that which he had preached in the past.

The United States Grand Jury at Springfield invited him to address the people of that city on the questions of the time. He spoke on the 12th of June, 1857, to a large and enthusiastic audience. He assured the people that he cordially accepted the decision and that it was in perfect harmony with his favorite doctrine of squatter sovereignty. The master's right to his slave in the Territories he admitted was guaranteed by the Constitution and neither Congress nor the legislature could interfere with it; yet practically this right was worthless unless sustained, protected and enforced by appropriate police regulations and local legislation prescribing adequate remedies for its violation. These regulations and remedies must depend entirely upon the will and wishes of the people of the Territory, as they could only be prescribed by the local legislature. Hence, the great principle of popular sovereignty and self-government was sustained and firmly established by the authority of the decision.

Perhaps, as pointed out by a recent historian, it would have been wiser for Douglas to have planted himself on the sound legal proposition that the only question decided by the Court was that it had no jurisdiction of the cause and that everything in the opinion beyond this was mere obiter dicta determining nothing. But it was no easy matter for a politician in 1857 to explain to a popular audience that a small fraction of the opinion of the highest Court was binding, while the remainder was merely the private opinion of the Judges on a matter not before them. Had Douglas been defending his opinions before a bench of trained jurists he might have safely rested his case on this sound but technical rule. He afterwards did so justify his opinions in the Senate. An experience politician determined to carry a popular election in a dangerous crisis might well hesitate to attempt so doubtful an experiment. History would have less temptation to call him a demagogue had he pursued that course. But we may well doubt whether, considered as a problem of practical politics, he was not wise in depending on his ingenious sophistry, rather than on this sound legal proposition.

Two weeks after his speech Lincoln addressed the people of Springfield in reply, pointing out the fallacy of Douglas' chief argument. But Lincoln was still an obscure lawyer; Douglas was the omnipotent Senator whose ipse dixit was final and carried conviction to the uncritical multitude.

Chapter XI. Popular Sovereignty in Congress.

While the Supreme Court was dedicating the Territories to slavery and Douglas was preaching local nullification, anarchy continued its delirious dance in Kansas. Guerilla warfare continued to vex the Territory as with unconscious humor the settlers illustrated the doctrine of popular sovereignty in practical operation.

On January 12th, 1857, the legislature met at Lecompton. On the same day the pro-slavery party held a convention in which it was decided that it was useless to continue the struggle. But the more active and determined leaders were not so easily discouraged and decided with the aid of the Administration to force a pro-slavery Constitution upon the people and drag the young Commonwealth into the Union as a slave State. By the middle of February a bill passed the legislature providing for the holding of a Constitutional Convention. It made no provision for submitting the Constitution to a vote. Governor Geary vetoed it. The bill was at once passed over the veto. The election of delegates to the Convention was set for the 15th of June.

Among the earliest acts of the new President was the appointment of Ex-Senator Robert J. Walker of Mississippi as Governor of the Territory. Before going to his post of duty, Walker visited Douglas at Chicago for counsel and showed him his inaugural address, in which he declared that any Constitution adopted must be submitted to a vote of the resident citizens of the Territory. Douglas heartily approved this and with all sincerity wished the new Governor God-speed in his perilous enterprise. Walker arrived late in May. In the name of the President he promised that the election of delegates to the Convention should be free from fraud and violence and that the Constitution should be fairly submitted to a vote. Buchanan assured him that on the question of submitting the Constitution to the bona fide resident settlers he was willing to stand or fall.

When the election was held the Republicans, who numbered at least two-thirds of the voters of the Territory, committed the blunder of refusing to vote. It was within their power to control the Convention and dictate the Constitution. But their bitter experience had produced utter distrust of the Federal Government and silent rebellion against it. They had organized themselves into a band of rebels bent on maintaining their free State. The election resulted in the choice of a majority of rabid pro-slavery delegates.

The Convention which met on October 19th produced a unique Constitution, declaring that the right of property was before and higher than any constitutional sanction, that the right of the owner of a slave to such slave and his increase was the same and as inviolable as the right of the owner of any property whatever, and provided that it could not be amended before 1865, and then could not interfere with slavery. With exquisite ingenuity it was decided to call an election on December 21st and let the people vote on the question whether they were "for the Constitution with slavery," or "for the Constitution with no slavery." No vote against the Constitution was permitted. To make assurance doubly sure, it was provided that, if "the Constitution with no slavery" carried, slavery should not exist in the State except that the right of property in slaves then in the Territory should in no measure be interfered with.

Walker denounced it as a fraud. Buchanan in his feeble way intended at fist to support him. But the Southern hotspurs, who understood the vacillating old man, threatened secession and general ruin unless he adopted their program. He yielded and threw the whole influence of his office for the admission of the State with this Constitution.

But this was too much for the patient Northern Democrats. Murmurs of criticism, swelling to shouts of denunciation, were heard in the North without much regard to politics. Douglas, who was in Chicago when the news arrived of the attempted swindle, immediately denounced it and promised his strenuous opposition. The situation of Kansas was tragical. But that of Douglas was still more so. He had staked his standing as a statesman upon the establishment of the right of the settlers to mould their own institutions and had successfully urged the election of Buchanan on the solemn pledge that the principle of popular sovereignty would be faithfully applied. He had reached the parting of the ways. At the last election Michigan had defeated Cass for his political sins and elected the radical Chandler in his place. Would Illinois' patience last forever? Was it certain that the cool, deep-plotting Lincoln would not succeed in overthrowing his power if he accepted the program of his party? He must stand for reelection next year and Illinois sentiment could not be trifled with now. The rebellion of Northern Democrats against Southern policies was not limited to Michigan. If he would be President, he must retain his Northern Democratic support. He would gladly have the South, but he must have Illinois. Already history has rendered a divided verdict upon this period of his life. He heartily abhorred the Kansas fraud and would really have liked to see the people given a fair chance to make a government for themselves. He believed in fair play and despised sharp practice and pettifogging tricks. He had the sincere faith in popular wisdom and virtue characteristic of the West. His cherished doctrine had been embodied in a ghastly abortion. His pledge to the people had been shamelessly broken. While the course of honor happened to be that of prudence, Douglas was not incapable of choosing it from pure and unselfish patriotism.

The people of Kansas, outraged by the proceedings of the Convention, in large numbers petitioned the Governor to call a special session of the legislature to remedy the wrong. He summoned it to meet December 7th and it at once ordered the whole Constitution submitted to the people on January 4th. The election ordered by the Convention was held on December 21st. The free-State people declined to vote. "The Constitution with slavery" carried by a vote of 6,143 to 589. On January 4th the pro-slavery men took part in the election of State officers, but refused to vote on the Constitution, holding that the legislature had no power to submit it. More than ten thousand votes were cast against the Constitution and another set of officers for an imaginary state selected.

The Constitution was sent to Buchanan to be submitted to Congress. This was the beginning of Douglas' official relation to the affair.

Congress met on the 5th of December. When Douglas reached Washington he called on the President to discuss the program for the winter. He told him that it would never do to send the Constitution to Congress for approval. It violated the plighted faith of the President and his party. His advice was that it be summarily rejected. Buchanan must submit it and recommend its approval. Douglas told him he would denounce it in the Senate. The President, excited and alarmed, rose from his seat and said, with great solemnity:

"Mr. Douglas, I desire you to remember that no Democrat ever yet differed from an Administration of his own choice without being crushed;" then he bade him beware of the fate of certain noted insurgents in the old Jackson-VanBuren days.

"Mr. President," replied Douglas, "I wish you to remember that General Jackson is dead."

On the 8th of December Buchanan transmitted his first message to Congress, which satisfied the world that he had abandoned such faint convictions as he had theretofore had and surrendered unconditionally to the South. He confessed that he had formerly pledged himself that the Constitution should be submitted to a vote of the people. But he said he had reached the conclusion that the only question upon which it was important to take the popular judgement was that of slavery. This question could not be more clearly or distinctly submitted than it would be under the ordinance of the Convention on December 21st. Should the Constitution without slavery be adopted, it, of course guarded the right of property in all slaves then in the Territory; but that was only common justice.

It was a great day in Washington. As a leading statesman declared, "the Administration had staked their all upon sustaining the Kansas Constitution, * * * * but Douglas was against it, decidedly, but not extravagantly." It was felt that a great storm was brewing, but of so uncertain and mysterious a character that no one knew what to expect. Douglas, who had theretofore scoffed at moral ideas in politics, had turned stern moralist, though still protesting his old cynical indifference, and was declaring inexpiable war on those whose champion he had been on a hundred hard fought fields. And strange to say, the allies with whom he was now to join hands, were Seward and Hale, perhaps even Chase and Sumner.

When the message was read on the 8th, he moved that 15,000 extra copies of it be printed for the use of the Senate and announced his intention to attack that part of it relating to Kansas. The next day when he rose to speak the galleries were thronged with an eager multitude. He congratulated the country that the President had not endorsed the Constitution or recommended its approval, but had only expressed his own satisfaction with it. He patronizingly apologized for Buchanan's error in supposing that the Kansas-Nebraska act provided only for the submission of the slavery question to a vote, recalling the fact that, at the time that act was passed he was representing the country with great wisdom and distinction at a foreign court and had never given the matter serious thought.

They had, in fact, repealed the Missouri Compromise and justified it everywhere on the ground that the people of the Territories had the right to form all their institutions according to their will. The President's later doctrine was in error, radical, fundamental, subversive of the platform on which he was elected. His suggestion that the Convention, throughout the territorial legislature, had the implied sanction of Congress, was without foundation. The Toombs bill expressly authorizing the calling of a Convention had recently passed the Senate, but was defeated in the House, clearly indicating that Congress disapproved it. The legislature could not give consent for Congress which it had itself refused. The Administration of Jackson solemnly decided in the case of Arkansas that a Territory had no right to hold a Constitutional Convention until Congress passed an act authorizing it. The Lecompton Convention differed from the Topeka Convention only in this; that the latter was called in opposition to the will of the legislature, while the former was sanctioned by it. But that body was utterly without authority in the matter until Congress empowered it to act.

When the delegates to this Convention were elected everyone supposed that their work would be submitted to a vote. The President and his Cabinet so understood it. Governor Walker so understood it and pledged his own word and that of the President that it would be submitted. A form of submission had been devised such that all men might come forward freely and vote for the Constitution and no man was permitted to vote against it. This resembled the French election when the First Consul sent the soldiers to the polls telling them to vote just as they pleased; but adding, "if you vote for Napoleon all is well; if you vote against him you will be shot." The objection to submitting the Constitution to a vote was that it would be voted down.

"Sir," he said, "my honor is pledged; and before it shall be tarnished I will take whatever consequences personal to myself may come; but never ask me to do an act which the President in his message has said is a forfeiture of faith, a violation of honor. * * * I will go as far as any of you to save the party. I have as much heart in the great cause that binds us together as any man living. I will sacrifice anything short of principle and honor for the peace of the party; but if the party will not stand by its principles, its faith, its pledges, I will stand there and abide whatever consequences may result from the position. * * * It is none of my business which way the slavery clause is decided. I care not whether it is voted up or voted down."

He urged the wisdom of passing a fair enabling act authorizing the people to hold a Constitutional Convention and providing for the submission of its work to the people and the orderly admission of the State. "But if this Constitution is to be forced down our throats," he continued, "in violation of the fundamental principles of free government, under a mode of submission that is a mockery and an insult, I will resist it to the last. I have no fear of any party associations being severed; * * * but if it must be, if I cannot act with you and preserve my faith and honor, I will stand on the great principle of popular sovereignty which declares the right of all people to be left perfectly free to form and regulate their institutions in their own way." This remarkable speech was recognized by all who heard it as marking an epoch, not merely in the life of the orator, but in the evolution of party politics at a time when parties were bending in death grapple and them most portentous civil war in history was looming in the distance. The speech was a clean, powerful, dispassionate argument delivered with an air of dignity and fortitude that greatly mollified the hearts of his old enemies.

Bigler of Pennsylvania, rising to defend the President, reminded the Senate that only a short year ago Douglas had voted for the Toombs bill, which provided for the holding of a Constitutional Convention without submitting its work to the people. Douglas protested that he did not so understand the bill and challenged Bigler for evidence that a single Senator so understood it. A remarkable dialogue followed. Bigler, who was a Democrat and a humble admirer of Douglas, said:

"I was present when that subject was discussed by Senators before the bill was introduced, and the question whether the Constitution when formed should be submitted to a vote of the people. It was held by those most intelligent on the subject that * * * it would be better that there should be no (such) provision in the Toombs bill; and it was my understanding * * * that the Convention would make a Constitution and send it here without submitting it to the popular vote."

Douglas inquired, angrily, whether he meant to insinuate that he had been present at any such conference. Bigler hesitated and sought to avoid the disclosure of the proceedings at their secret caucus, but Douglas impetuously released him from all secrecy and challenged him, if he knew, to declare, that, directly or indirectly, publicly or privately, anywhere on the face of the earth, he was ever present at such a consultation when it was called to his attention and he agreed to approve a Constitution without submitting it to the people.

Bigler, who had an uneasy suspicion that he was improperly disclosing party secrets, could not decline the challenge, and replied that he remembered very well that the question was discussed at a conference held at Douglas' own house. "It was then urged," he said, "by Toombs, that there should be no provision for the submission of the Constitution to the people." He did not remember whether Douglas took part in the discussion, but his own understanding of the sense of the caucus was that the Convention should have the right to make a Constitution and send it directly to Congress for approval.

Douglas protested that he was innocent of any such conspiracy. He confessed that his attention was called to the fact that no provision was made in the Toombs bill for the submission of the Constitution, but his understanding was that, powers not delegated being reserved, it would, of course, be submitted. Bigler reminded him that, while he had taken this for granted in the case of Kansas, he had about the same time drafted a bill for the admission of Minnesota in which he took care to provide in express terms that the Constitution must be submitted. If he then thought general principles of law secured the submission of the Kansas Constitution without providing for it in the enabling act, why this care to expressly provide for it in the Minnesota act?

He was now swimming amid perilous breakers. He had thrown down the gage of battle to his party. In the twinkling of an eye he was transformed from recognized chief to a rebel; but he was isolated and unsupported. He could not consort with Republicans. The rankling wounds of the by-gone years could not heal so suddenly. Moreover, he did not want their society. He intended to remain a Democrat and hoped to force upon his party such policies that Illinois and the Northwest would be solidly at his back. With the Democratic States of the North standing firmly with him he could still dictate terms to the South, which would have to choose between Northern Democrats and Northern Republicans.

Chapter XII. The Lecompton Constitution.

On February 2nd Buchanan sent to Congress his message, transmitting the Lecompton Constitution and urging its approval. As apology for his change of front and excuse for a like change in others he drew a dark picture of the disturbed condition of affairs in the Territory, portraying the Topeka free State enterprise as a vast insurrectionary movement. He told Congress that it was impossible to submit the whole instrument to a vote because the free State faction, who were the majority, would vote against any Constitution, however perfect, except their own. He commended the entire regularity of the Lecompton Convention and the fairness with which the slavery question had been submitted to a vote and urged immediate admission.

When the motion to print and refer to the Committee on Territories was made, Trumbull denounced the message with great energy and at some length. He asked sneeringly what had become of the once celebrated principle of popular sovereignty? The people of Kansas were denied the right of voting on their Constitution at all and the Dred Scott decision had settled that at no stage had the people of a Territory power to interfere with slavery. The whole doctrine, he declared, had been absolutely repudiated.

The message having been referred to the Committee on Territories after six days' debate, on the 18th of February a bill was reported by a majority of the Committee for the admission of Kansas into the Union under the Lecompton Constitution and Douglas presented a minority report protesting against it. For two weeks he was confined to his room by sickness, but, as the day for the vote was near, notice was given that he would speak on the 22nd of March.

On that day the Senate met at the early hour of ten. Already the galleries were crowded. Long before noon the passages leading to the Chamber were thronged with men and women vainly seeking admission. In a moment of graceful gallantry the Senators admitted the ladies to the floor. Through long hours of debate the crowd waited. The Senate adjourned until seven o'clock, at which time Douglas was to speak. The visitors who were lucky enough to have gained admission waited with patient good humor for the return of the Senators, who at last began to force their way back into the Chamber through the dense throngs.

A little before seven the short figure of Douglas was observed at the door and he was greeted with loud applause from the galleries. The session resumed and he rose to speak. Cheered as he was by the sympathy and admiration of the visitors, it was to him a stern enough hour when he must finally break with his powerful party and battle with his utmost strength against its cherished program. He must attack, not Buchanan, but the organized Democracy, now more powerfully entrenched than ever before. It controlled the President and the Supreme Court and had bent them to its will in this precise quarrel. The Senate was Democratic nearly two to one, and but two of the majority followed him in his revolt. In the House the Democrats had a majority of twenty-five.

Foreseeing the personal consequences of his act, he opened his speech with an elaborate review of his course in Congress in relation to slavery in the Territories, showing that from the beginning he had favored leaving the whole question fairly to the inhabitants. He stood on the principle of the Compromise of 1850 as approved and interpreted by the legislature of Illinois in 1851. That body had declared that the people of a Territory had a right to form such government as they chose. But was the Lecompton Constitution the act and deed of the people of Kansas? Did it embody their will? If not, Congress had no right to impose it on them. Where was the evidence that it did embody their will? By a fraudulent vote on December 12th it was adopted by 5,500 majority. By a fair vote on January 4th it was defeated by 10,000 majority. The election on December 21st was ordered by the Lecompton Convention, deriving its authority from the territorial legislature. The legislature itself ordered the election on January 4th. Granting the argument that the organic act was in effect an enabling act, then the territorial legislature had power to authorize the Lecompton Convention and also to order it work submitted to a vote. The legislature either had the full power of Congress over the subject or it had none.

But, it was claimed, the Constitution would have been voted down if submitted. What right had Congress to force it upon the people? It was a mockery to call it an embodiment of their will and a crime to attempt to enforce it. If it ever became the Constitution of Kansas it would be the act of Congress that made it so and not the decision of the people. That it could be changed thereafter was no apology for this outrage. It was as much a violation of fundamental principle, a violation of popular sovereignty, to force a Constitution on an unwilling people for a day as for a year or for a longer time.

If a few thousand Free Soilers had fabricated a Constitution in this fashion, prohibiting slavery forever, would the gentlemen from the South have submitted to the outrage? They were asked to admit Kansas with a State government brought into existence not only by fraudulent voting but forged returns sustained by perjury.

He paused to comment on certain diatribes in the Washington Union which had denounced him as a renegade, traitor and deserter, and read from its columns an article presenting the extreme claims of the South, arguing that all laws and Constitutions of the free States forbidding slavery were violations of the Federal Constitution, and that the emancipation of slaves in the Northern States was a gross outrage on the rights of property. But this article, he said, was in harmony with the Lecompton Constitution, which declared the right of property in a slave to be higher than Constitutions. This meant that the Constitutions of the free States forbidding slavery were in conflict with the Constitution of the United States and of no validity. Hence slavery had right to exist in all the States. But this was not the authentic Democratic faith, which left the whole question to the option of the several States. If each one took care of its own affairs, minded its own business and let its neighbors alone, there would be peace in the country. Seward had proclaimed a higher law which forbade slavery everywhere. this instrument and the Administration paper proclaimed a higher law which established it in all the States. It was time to quit this folly and yield obedience to the Constitution and laws of the land.

It was the most arrant presumption for the Administration to attempt to make this a party measure. By what right did these accidental and temporary holders of office prescribe party politics? There had been no Convention, not even a caucus, since this question arose. The party was not committed. The President had no right to tell a Senator his duty and command his allegiance. He had no power to prescribe tests. A Senator's first duty was to his State. "If the will of my State is one way and the will of the President is the other, am I to be told that I must obey the Executive and betray my State, or else be branded as a traitor to the party and hunted down by all the newspapers that share the patronage of the Government? And every man who holds a petty office in any part of my State to have the question put to him, 'Are you Douglas' enemy? If not, your head comes off.'"

What despotism on earth could equal this? The obedience of Senators was demanded on this question only. On all else they were free. The President was evidently guided by the old adage that a man needs no friends when he knows he is right and only want his friends to stand by him when he is wrong.

The President regretted that the Constitution was not submitted to the people, although he knew that if it had been submitted it would have been rejected. Hence, he regretted that it had not been rejected. Would he regret that it had not been submitted and rejected if he did not think it was wrong? And yet, he demanded their assistance in forcing it on an unwilling people and threatened vengeance on all who refused.

"For my part," he continued, * * * "come what may, I intend to vote, speak and act according to my own sense of duty, so long as I hold a seat in this Chamber. * * * I have no professions to make of my fidelity. I have no vindication to make of my course. Let it speak for itself. * * * I intend to perform my duty in accordance with my own convictions. Neither the frowns of power nor the influence of patronage will change my action, nor drive me from my principles. I stand firmly and immovably upon those great principles of self-government and State sovereignty upon which the campaign was fought and won. I stand by the time honored principles of the Democratic party, illustrated by Jefferson and Jackson, those principles of State rights, of State sovereignty, of strict construction, upon which the great Democratic party has ever stood. I will stand by the Constitution of the United States with all its compromises and perform all my obligations under it. I will stand by the American Union as it exists under the Constitution. If standing firmly by my principles I shall be driven into private life, it is a fate that has no terrors for me. * * * If the alternative be private life or servile obedience to the Executive will, I am prepared to retire. Official position has no charm for me when deprived of that freedom of thought and action which becomes a gentleman and a Senator."

When he closed, Toombs rose to reply. The speech was offensively bitter and personal, in one memorable passage of which he announced that the slave States would take care of themselves and were prepared to bid defiance to the North and to the world. Green of Missouri answered in coarser strain, both intimating that Douglas had been guilty of deliberate perfidy in his change of front.

On the 23rd the vote was taken and the bill passed, 33 being for it and 25 against it.

The Administration now declared war on him. The patronage was unsparingly used against his friends and it was better for an applicant for Federal appointment to be accused of any crime than suspected of friendship with Douglas. This separation from his party touched his feelings more deeply than any other event of his life, and we find surprising evidence of his being shaken by deep emotions that seem out of harmony with his robust and unsentimental nature. But when we remember that all his life had been spent in the activities of politics, that his thoughts, sentiments and passions had all been political for twenty years, that the Democratic platform was at once his creed and his philosophy, we can understand something of the choking emotion that threatened to overpower him as he announced that he was thenceforth a rebel and a heretic. After December 9th, the Administration press attacked him bitterly and he found himself everywhere proclaimed a traitor and deserter. He told the Senate that he knew the knife would be put to the throats of his followers. The Administration Senators assailed him. But he was equal to all emergencies and his new position as the recognized leader of the anti-Lecompton revolt gave him the enthusiastic applause of the Northwest.

On March 23rd the bill went to the House. A motion was made to refer it to a special committee. A contest over this motion arose, lasted all night, and degenerated into a general brawl, in which a Member from Pennsylvania knocked down a South Carolina Member, and many others were engaged in fisticuffs. At last a reference was agreed to.

On April 1st, while the House had the bill under consideration, Montgomery of Pennsylvania offered a substitute which had been offered by Crittenden in the Senate and there rejected, providing that the Constitution should be submitted to a vote, and, if adopted, the President should at once proclaim the admission of the State; if rejected, the inhabitants should hold a new Constitutional Convention.

This substitute passed the House but was rejected by the Senate. A conference Committee was appointed, which reported the notorious English bill, providing that a generous grant of land should be offered to Kansas, and the people at a special election vote to accept it. If they so voted, they were to be admitted as a State with the Lecompton Constitution. If they rejected the grant, they could not be admitted until they numbered 93,000, which meant indefinite postponement. The bill was merely an offer of a bribe to the people to accept a Constitution which they abhorred. Its form was such that men who still believe it well to maintain the guise of decency could vote for it on the pretence that it was a land grant.

Douglas, who had now tried the thorny path of rebellion, faltered. He was tempted to support the bill and seek reconciliation, but decided to vote against it. It passed the Senate by a majority of nine and the House by a majority of eight. In the following August the proposition was submitted and rejected so decisively that the maddest fanatic must have seen that all hope of making Kansas a slave State was gone forever.

Chapter XIII. The Illinois Campaign.

Congress adjourned on June 16th and Douglas, after spending a few days in New York, returned to Chicago. Meanwhile the people of Illinois had awakened to great political activity. On April 21st the regular Democratic Convention was held at Springfield and without opposition passed a resolution endorsing his candidacy for re-election. On June 9th the "Administration Democracy," consisting of the Federal office holders and those democrats who condemned his anti-Lecompton battle, held a Convention at Springfield, the purpose of which was to divide the party and insure his defeat. On the 17th the Republicans held their Convention at Springfield and chose Lincoln as their candidate for United States Senator.

The nomination of Lincoln was not an accident. He was prepared to accept it in a speech that should serve as the text of his campaign and was destined to great fame in after years. Against the resolve of his friends he announced the dangerous doctrine that the Government could not endure permanently half slave and half free. "A house divided against itself cannot stand." He did not expect the Union to be dissolved or the house to fall, but that it would cease to be divided. "Either the opponents of slavery will arrest the further spread of it, and place it where the public mind shall rest in the belief that it is in the course of ultimate extinction, or its advocates will push it forward till it shall become alike lawful in all the States, old as well as new, North as well as South."

The repeal of the Missouri Compromise and the establishment of squatter sovereignty was a great step towards the nationalization of slavery. This was followed by the Dred Scott decision forbidding Congress to interfere with it in the Territories. All the legislation of Congress had carefully reserved a place for this expected decision. Douglas had hinted it in the Senate long before it was announced. Pierce and Buchanan had proclaimed it before the Judges. "We cannot absolutely know that all these exact adaptations are the result of preconcert. But when we see a lot of framed timbers, different portions of which we know have been gotten out at different times and different place, and by different workmen,--Stephen, Franklin, Roger and James, for instance,--and when we see these timbers all joined together and see they exactly make the frame of a house or mill, all the tenons and mortises exactly fitting, * * * * * we find it impossible not to believe that Stephen and Franklin and Roger and James all understood one another from the beginning and all worked upon a common plan or draft drawn up before the first blow was struck."

He repelled the suggestion made in some quarters that the Republicans ought to cease their fight on Douglas and rally to his support in his contest with the slavery propagandists. He reminded them that the very essence of Republican faith was hostility to slavery, while Douglas frankly declared that he did not care whether it was voted up or voted down. The cause must be entrusted to those whose hearts were in the work and who did care for the result.

On the 9th of July Douglas returned to Chicago and received a royal welcome. A special train loaded with prominent citizens was dispatched to meet him. On his arrival he was greeted with tumultuous applause. He addressed the vast multitude from the balcony of the Tremont House. Thirty thousand people are said to have gathered to hear him. He was profoundly pleased by this splendid ovation so strikingly in contrast with the reception four years before, when his neighbors refused even to hear him in defense of his course. Among the distinguished visitors on the speakers' stand sat Lincoln.

After thanking his audience for the enthusiastic reception, he plunged into the subject then uppermost in the public mind by rehearsing his relation to the whole Kansas problem. He reminded them of his early and consistent devotion to popular sovereignty, which had been so utterly outraged by the Lecompton Constitution. He assured his hearers, however, that his opposition to that Constitution arose from no sentimental morality and bore no relation to the ethics of slavery. He insisted, not that it be good or just, but that it be submitted to a vote of the settlers.

He then addressed himself to Lincoln's Springfield speech. He attacked his extreme doctrines with characteristic adroitness. Lincoln's speech was of doubtful prudence as a campaign argument. It really foreboded civil war or a peaceful dissolution of the Union. While this alternative was, perhaps, inevitable, political expediency forbade its avowal. Douglas declared the necessary result of his philosophy to be a war of sections, a war of the North against the South, of the free States against the slave States, to be continued relentlessly until the one or the other should be subdued and all should either become free States or all become slave States. But this was not the true theory of the American Union. The States differed widely in soil, climate, resources, tastes and habits. Their laws and institutions were utterly unlike. New Hampshire's laws were unfit for South Carolina; those of New York were not suited to the Pacific Coast. Uniformity in local and domestic affairs would be destructive of State rights, State sovereignty and personal liberty. Uniformity was the parent of despotism the world over. The only way of attaining Lincoln's proposed uniformity would be to abolish State legislatures, blot out State sovereignty and merge the States into one consolidated empire. But diversity, dissimilarity, variety in all their local and domestic institutions was the great safeguard of their liberties. He insisted on reverently bowing to the Supreme Court as the authoritative expounder of the Constitution, rather than appealing from it to a tumultuous town meeting where constitutional questions arose. The Federal Government was founded on the white basis. It was made by white men, for the benefits of white men, to be administered by white men in such manner as they should determine. Let each State decide for itself how it would treat the negroes and let its neighbors alone.

"The issues between Mr. Lincoln and myself," he said, "are made up, * * * *. He goes for uniformity in our domestic institutions, for a war of sections, until one or the other shall be subdued. I go for * * * the right of the people to decide for themselves. On the other hand Mr. Lincoln goes for a warfare on the Supreme Court. * * * * I yield obedience to the decisions of that Court. * * * * I am opposed to negro equality. I repeat that this nation is a white people, * * * * a people that have established this Government for themselves and their posterity. * * * * I am opposed to taking any step that recognizes the negro man * * * as the equal of the white man. I am opposed to giving him a voice in the administration of the Government."

The reception was recognized by the politicians of both parties as a great success. It was a brilliant opening of the senatorial campaign. The Republicans were anxious to counteract it. On the following evening Lincoln spoke at the same place.

He had a large and enthusiastic audience. But he was not an impromptu orator at all comparable to Douglas. While his carefully prepared Springfield speech was decidedly better than Douglas' dashing address in Chicago, his unprepared speech was by no means equal to it. The marked disparity between the two speeches must have intensified the suspicion among Lincoln's friends that he was no match for his rival on the stump.

On the 16th of July Douglas again spoke to a vast multitude at Bloomington. He made an artful appeal for the Whig vote by a well turned compliment to "Kentucky's great and gallant statesman, John J. Crittenden," who proposed to refer the whole question back to the people of Kansas and thus "showed himself a worthy successor of the immortal Clay." The Republicans had "endorsed the great principle of the Kansas-Nebraska bill," they had "come to the Douglas platform in supporting the Crittenden-Montgomery bill." The compromise of 1850 embodied the principle that every people ought to have the privilege of forming and regulating their own institutions to suit themselves. Each State had that right and no reason existed why it should not be extended to the Territories. The Illinois House of Representatives by an almost unanimous vote had asserted that the principle embodied in the measures of 1850 was the birth-right of free men, the gift of heaven, a principle vindicated by our Revolutionary fathers, that no limitation should ever be placed upon it either in the organization of a territorial government or the admission of a State into the Union. In conformity with that principle he had brought in the Kansas-Nebraska bill, for which Lincoln and his friends were seeking his defeat.

"I have known Lincoln well," he said, "for a quarter of a century. I have known him as you all know him, a kind-hearted, amiable gentleman, a right good fellow, a worthy citizen, of eminent ability as a lawyer, and, I have no doubt, sufficient ability to make a good Senator."

He examined Lincoln's "house divided-against-itself" philosophy, pointing out that the house had been divided for nearly seventy years and still stood.

"How is Lincoln, if elected Senator, going to carry out that principle which he says is essential to the existence of this Union; that slavery must be abolished in all the States, or must be established in all? * * * * He invites, by his proposition, a war between Illinois and Kentucky, a war between the free States and the slave States, a war between the North and the South, for the purpose of either exterminating slavery in every Southern State, or planting it in every Northern State. * * * * * What man in Illinois would not lose the last drop if his heart's blood before he would submit to the institution of slavery being forced upon us by the other States against our will? * * * What Southern man would not shed the last drop of his heart's blood to prevent Illinois or any other Northern State from interfering to abolish slavery in his State? * * * * I am opposed to organizing a sectional party which appeals to Northern pride and Northern passion and prejudice against Southern institutions, thus stirring up ill feeling and hot blood between brethren of the same Republic. * * * * How is he to carry out his principles when he gets to the Senate? Does he intend to introduce a bill to abolish slavery in Kentucky? Does he intend to introduce a bill to interfere with slavery in Virginia? How is he to accomplish what he professes must be done to save the Union?

"There would be but one way to carry out his ideas. That would be to establish a consolidated empire as destructive to the liberties of the people and the rights of the citizen as that of Austria or Russia or any other despotism that rests upon the necks of the people * * * *. Who among you expects to live or have his children live until slavery shall be established in Illinois or abolished in South Carolina? * * * * There is but one possible way in which slavery can be abolished and that is by leaving a State * * * * perfectly free to form and regulate its institutions in its own way. That was the principle upon which this Republic was founded. * * * * Under its operation slavery disappeared from New Hampshire, from Rhode Island, from Connecticut, from New York, from New Jersey, from Pennsylvania, from six of the twelve original slave holding States; and this gradual emancipation went on so long as we in the free states minded our own business and left our neighbors alone, * * * * so long as the free States were content with managing their own affairs and leaving the South perfectly free to do as they pleased. But the moment the North said, 'We are powerful enough to control you of the South,' * * * * that moment the South combined to resist the attack and thus sectional parties were formed and gradual emancipation ceased in all the Northern slave holding States * * *.

"Lincoln makes another issue, * * * * a crusade against the Supreme Court of the United Sates because of its decision in the Dred Scott case. * * * * I have no crusade to preach against that august body. * * * * I receive the decision of the Judges of that Court when pronounced as the final adjudication upon all questions within their jurisdiction. * * * * Unless we respect and bow in deference to the final decisions of the highest judicial tribunal in our country, we are driven at once to anarchy, to violence, to mob law, and there is no security left for our property or our own civil rights. * * * * Are we to appeal from the Supreme Court to a country meeting like this? * * * Does Mr. Lincoln intend to appeal from the decision of the Supreme Court to a Republican caucus or a town meeting? * * * He tells you that he is opposed to the decision in the Dred Scott case. Well, suppose he is; what is he going to do about it? I never got beat in a law suit in my life that I was not opposed to the decision. * * * * This Government is divided into three separate and distinct branches. * * * * Each one is supreme within the circle of its own powers. The functions of Congress are to enact the statutes, the province of the Court is to pronounce upon their validity, and the duty of the Executive is to carry the decision into effect."

Yet, he said, Lincoln wants to be elected Senator in order to reverse the Dred Scott decision by passing another unconstitutional statute. He can not get rid of the Judges now on the bench until they die. He must first elect a Republican President by Northern votes bound by pledges to appoint none but Republicans to the bench. He must then persuade the Judges to die. The President must pledge his new Judges in advance to decide this slavery question according to the wishes of his party, regardless of the Constitution. What confidence would the people have in a Court thus constituted?--a Court composed of partisan Judges, appointed on political grounds, catechized in advance and pledged in regard to a decision before the argument and without reference to the state of facts? Would such a Court command the respect of the country? Without regard to the Dred Scott decision slavery will go just where the people want it and not one inch further.

"I tell you, my friends, it is impossible under our institutions to force slavery on an unwilling people. If this principle of popular sovereignty * * * be fairly carried out by letting the people decide the question for themselves by a fair vote at a fair election and with honest returns, slavery will never exist one day or one hour in any Territory against the unfriendly legislation of an unfriendly people. I care not how the Dred Scott decision may have settled the abstract question so far as the practical results are concerned. * * * If the people of the Territory want slavery they will encourage it by passing affirmatory laws and the necessary police regulations, patrol laws and slave code; if they do not want it they will withhold that legislation and by withholding it slavery is a dead as if prohibited by a constitutional provision. * * * * * They could pass such local laws as would drive slavery out in one day or one hour, if they were opposed to it; and therefore, so far as the question of slavery in the Territory is concerned, so far as the principle of popular sovereignty is concerned in its practical operation, it matters not how the Dred Scott case may be decided. * * * * * Whether slavery shall exist or shall not exist in any State or Territory will depend on whether the people are for or against it; and which ever way they shall decide it will be entirely satisfactory to me."

The Dred Scott case, he continued, decides that negroes are not citizens. But Lincoln insists on conferring on them all the privileges, rights and immunities of citizens. "I believe this Government of ours was founded on the white basis. I believe it was established for white men, of the benefit of white men and their posterity in all time to come. I do not believe that it was the design or intention of the signers of the Declaration of Independence or the framers of the Constitution to include negroes as citizens. * * * The position Lincoln has taken on this question not only presents him as claiming for them the right to vote, but their right under the divine law and the Declaration of Independence to be elected to office, to become members of the legislature, to go to Congress, to become Governors or United States Senators, or Judges of the Supreme Court. * * * He would permit them to marry, would he not? And if he gives them that right I suppose he will let them marry whom they please, provided they marry their equals. If the divine law declares that the white man is the equal of the negro woman, that they are on a perfect equality, I suppose he admits the right of the negro woman to marry the white man. * * * I do not believe that the signers of the Declaration had any reference to negroes when they used the expression that all men were created equal. * * * They were speaking only of the white race. * * * Every one of the thirteen colonies was a slave-holding constituency. Did they intend * * * to declare that their own slaves were on an equality with them? What are the negroes' rights and privileges? That is a question which each State and Territory must decide for itself. We have decided that question. We have said that in this State the negro shall not be a slave but that he shall enjoy no political rights; that negro equality shall not exist. * * * For my own part, I do not consider the negro any kin to me nor to any other white man; but I would still carry my humanity and philanthropy to the extent of giving him every privilege and every immunity that he could enjoy consistent with our own good."

Maine allows the negro to vote on an equality with the white man. New York permits him to vote, provided he owns $250 worth of property. In Kentucky they deny the negro all political and civil rights. Each is a sovereign State and has a right to do as it pleases. Let us mind our own business and not interfere with them. Lincoln is not going into Kentucky, but will plant his batteries on this side of the Ohio and throw his bomb shells--his Abolition documents--over the River and will carry on the political warfare and get up strife between the North and South until he elects a sectional President, reduces the South to the condition of dependent colonies, raises the negro to an equality and forces the South to submit to the doctrine that a house divided against itself cannot stand; that the Union divided into half slave States and half free cannot endure; that they must be all free or all slave; and that, as we in the North are in the majority, we will not permit them to be all slave and therefore they in the South must consent to the States being all free.

"These are my views and these are the principles to which I have devoted all my energies since 1850, when I acted side by side with the immortal Clay and the god-like Webster in that memorable struggle in which the Whigs and the Democrats united upon a common platform of patriotism and the Constitution. * * * And when I stood beside the death-bed of Mr. Clay and heard him refer with feelings and emotions of the deepest solicitude to the welfare of the country, and saw that he looked upon the principle embodied in the great Compromise of 1850, the principle of the Nebraska bill, the doctrine of leaving each State and Territory free to decide its institutions for itself, as the only means by which the peace of the country could be preserved and the Union perpetuated. I pledged him on that death-bed of his that so long as I lived my energy should be devoted to the vindication of that principle and of his fame as connected with it. I gave the same pledge to the great expounder of the Constitution, he who has been called the god-like Webster. I looked up to Clay and him as a son would to a father, and I call upon the people of Illinois and the people of the whole Union to bear testimony that never since the sod has been laid upon the graves of these eminent statesmen have I failed on any occasion to vindicate the principle with which the last great crowning acts of their lives were identified. * * * And now my life and energy are devoted to this work as the means of preserving this Union. * * * It can be maintained by preserving the sovcreignty of the States, the right of each State and each Territory to settle its domestic concerns for itself and the duty of each to refrain from interfering with the other in any of its local or domestic institutions. Let that be done, and the Union will be perpetuated. Let that be done, and this Republic which began with thirteen States and which now numbers thirty-two, which when it began only extended from the Atlantic to the Mississippi, but now reaches to the Pacific, may yet expand north and south until it covers the whole continent and becomes one vast, ocean-bound Confederacy. * * * * Let us maintain the great principles of popular sovereignty, of State rights and of the Federal Union as the Constitution has made it, and this Republic will endure forever."

On the following day he spoke at Springfield, repeating his Bloomington speech with slight abridgment.

In the evening, Lincoln, who had attended Douglas' Bloomington meeting and accompanied him to Springfield, spoke to a large audience. He twitted him for his noisy, spectacular campaign, "the thunderings of cannon, the marching and music, the fizzle-gigs and fireworks. * * *

"Does Judge Douglas," he asked, "when he says that several of the past years of his life have been devoted to the question of popular sovereignty and that all the remainder of his life shall be devoted to it, mean to say that he has been devoting his life to securing to the people of the territories the right to exclude slavery? * * * He and every one knows that the decision of the Supreme Court, which he approves and makes a special ground of attack upon me for disapproving, forbids the people of a Territory to exclude slavery. This covers the whole ground from the settlement of a Territory till it reaches the degree of maturity entitling it to form a State Constitution. So far as all that ground is concerned, the Judge is not sustaining popular sovereignty, but absolutely opposing it. He sustains the decision which declares that the popular will of the Territory has no constitutional power to exclude slavery during their territorial existence. This being so, the period of time from the first settlement of the Territory till it reaches the point of forming a State Constitution is not the thing that the Judge is fighting for; but, on the contrary, he is fighting for the thing that annihilates and crushes out that same popular sovereignty. * * * He is contending for the right of the people, when they come to make a State Constitution, to make it for themselves and precisely as best suits themselves.

That is quixotic. Nobody is opposing or has opposed the right of the people when they form a Constitution to form it for themselves. This being so, what is he going to spend his life for? Is he going to spend it in maintaining a principle that nobody on earth opposes? Does he expect to stand up in majestic dignity and go through this apothesis and become a god in maintaining a principle that neither man nor mouse in all God's creation opposes? * * * What is there in the opposition of Judge Douglas to the Lecompton Constitution that entitles him to be considered the only opponent to it, * * * the very quintessence of that opposition? * * *

He in the Senate and his class of men there formed the number of about twenty. It took one hundred and twenty to defeat the measure. There were six Americans and ninety-four Republicans. Why is it that twenty should be entitled to all the credit for doing that work and the hundred to none? Does he place his superior claim to credit on the ground that he has performed a good act that was never expected of him? Perhaps he places himself somewhat on the ground of the parable of the lost sheep which went astray upon the mountains, and when the owner of the hundred sheep found the one that was lost, there was more rejoicing over the one sheep that was lost and had been found than over the ninety-and-nine in the fold."

In opposing the Dred Scott decision, he said, he was sustained by the authority of Mr. Jefferson, who denounced the doctrine that the Judges were the ultimate arbiters of all constitutional questions as dangerous and tending to oligarchic despotism and insisted that, while they were as honest as other men, they were not more so, having the common passion for party, for power and the privilege of their crops, and ought not to be trusted with the dangerous power of deciding the great questions of State. The Supreme Court once decided that the national back was constitutional. The Democratic party revolted against the decision. Jackson himself asserted that he would not hold a national back to be constitutional, even though the Court had decided it to be so. The declaration that Congress had not power to establish a bank was contained in every Democratic platform since that time, in defiance of the solemn ruling of the Court. In fact, they had reduced the decision to an absolute nullity. And still Douglas boasted in the very speeches in which he denounced others for opposing the Dred Scott decision that he stood on the Cincinnati platform which repudiated and condemned the old bank decision.

He was for Supreme Court decisions when he liked them and against them when he did not like them. Would he not graciously allow the Republicans to do with the Dred Scott decision what they did with the bank decision?

Springfield was Lincoln's home. He knew his audience and met it with confidence. He now felt that he was Douglas' equal in the field in which he had hitherto eclipsed all rivals.

But it was evident that the current was running with Douglas. The great reception at Chicago had been a glorious opening. His journeys through the State were triumphal processions. Special trains, splendidly decorated, were at his service. Military escorts received him with the firing of cannon and the loud music of bands. He commanded and marshaled with the skill of a great artist all the pomp and circumstance of victory. He owned much property in Chicago, which with the growth of the city had greatly increased in value. He mortgaged this for campaign funds, borrowing eighty thousand dollars, a debt that harassed him to the grave. Wealthy friends contributed freely and the campaign was run regardless of expense.

Yet with all these advantages the contest was evidently a hard one. Two years before, the combined Republicans and Whigs of the State outnumbered the Democrats by nearly thirty thousand. The Whig party was breaking up. It was a serious question of practical politics whether they would drift to the Democrats or the Republicans. Illinois comprised two utterly distinct communities. The northern part of the State was settled by people from New England and the Northwest. The Southern part was settled from Kentucky and the other Southern States. The growth of Chicago and the rapid development of the northern counties had made the State extremely doubtful even for Douglas. To any other man his task was hopeless. In the north the anti-slavery sentiment was strong, even to fanaticism, and many of his own supporters prayed fervently for the arrival of the day when slavery would be blotted from existence. In the south, though slavery was prohibited by law, it was cherished in the hearts of the people who remembered with warm affection the old homesteads in Kentucky and Tennessee.

Lincoln had, with more frankness than discretion announced his views on the great question. It was supremely important to compel Douglas to explicitly declare himself, to hold him down to the dangerous issue and force him to speak plainly.

Each had the disadvantage of pleasing one section of the State at the cost of offending the other section. But Douglas was further embarrassed by the necessity of avoiding offense to the slave holding States of the South. He was a candidate not only for the Senate, but also for the Presidency.

Chapter XIV. The Debates with Lincoln.

Chicago, Ill., July 24, 1858. "Hon. S. A. Douglas:

"My dear Sir:--Will it be agreeable to you to make an arrangement for you and myself to divide time and address the same audiences the present canvass? Mr. Judd, who will hand you this, is authorized to receive your answer; and, if agreeable to you, to enter into the terms of such an arrangement.

"Your obedient servant,

"A. Lincoln."

This is the note received by Douglas a week after his return from Springfield. On the same day he returned the following answer:

"Chicago, Ill., July 24, 1858. "Hon. A. Lincoln:

"Dear Sir:--Your note of this date * * * was handed me by Mr. Judd. * * * I went to Springfield last week for the purpose of conferring with the Democratic State Central Committee upon the mode of conducting the canvass, and with them * * * made a list of appointments covering the entire period until late in October. The people of the several localities have been notified of the times and places of the meetings. * * * I cannot refrain from expressing my surprise, if it was your original intention to invite such an arrangement, that you should have waited until after I had made my appointments, in as much as we were both here in Chicago together for several days after my arrival, and again at Bloomington, Atlanta, Lincoln and Springfield, where it was well known I went for the purpose of consulting with the State Central Committee and agreeing upon the plan of campaign. * * * I will, in order to accommodate you, as far as it is in my power to do so, take the responsibility of making an arrangement with you for a discussion between us at one prominent point in each congressional district in the State, except the Second and Sixth, where we have both spoken and in each of which you had the concluding speech.

If agreeable to you, I will indicate the following places as the most suitable in the several congressional districts at which we should speak, to wit: Freeport, Ottawa, Galesburg, Quincy, Alton, Jonesboro and Charleston. * * *

"Very respectfully, your most obedient servant,

"S. A. Douglas."

Lincoln replied:

"Springfield, July 29, 1858.

"Hon. S. A. Douglas:

Dear Sir:--Yours of the 24th in relation to an arrangement to divide time and address the same audiences, is received; and, in apology for not sooner replying, allow me to say that, when I sat by you at dinner yesterday, I was not aware that you had answered my note, nor, certainly, that my own note had been presented to you. An hour after, I saw a copy of your answer in the Chicago Times, and reaching home I found the original awaiting me. * * * As to your surprise that I did not sooner make the proposal to divide time with you, I can only say, I made it as soon as I resolved to make it. I did not know but that such a proposal would come from you; I waited respectfully to see. * * * I agree to an arrangement for us to speak at the seven places you have named and at your own times, provided you name the times at once, so that I, as well as you, can have to myself the time not covered by the arrangement. As to the other details, I wish perfect reciprocity, and no more. I wish as much time as you and that conclusions shall alternate. That is all.

"Your obedient servant,

"A. Lincoln."

On the next day Douglas wrote:

"Bement, Piatt Co., Ill., July 30, 1858.

"Dear Sir:--Your letter, dated yesterday, accepting my proposition for a joint discussion at one prominent point in each congressional district * * * was received this morning. The times and places designated are as follows:

Ottawa, La Salle County .... August 21, 1858. Freeport, Stephenson County ..... August 27, 1858. Jonesboro, Union County ...... September 15, 1858. Charleston, Coles County ..... September 18, 1858. Galesburgh, Knox County .... October 7, 1858. Quincy, Adams County .... October 13, 1858. Alton, Madison County .... October 15, 1858.

"I agree to your suggestion that we shall alternately open and close the discussion. I will speak at Ottawa one hour, you can reply, occupying an hour and a half, and I will then follow for half an hour. At Freeport, you shall open the discussion and speak one hour; I will follow for an hour and a half, and you can then reply for half an hour. We will alternate in like manner in each successive place.

"Very respectfully, your obedient servant,

"S. A. Douglas."

To which Lincoln replied:

"Springfield, July 31, 1858.

"Hon. S. A. Douglas:

"Dear Sir:--Yours of yesterday, naming places, time and terms for joint discussions, between us, was received this morning. Although by the terms as you propose, you take four openings and closes to my three, I accede, and thus close the arrangement. * * *

"Your obedient servant,

"A. Lincoln."

Now that Lincoln has become idealized and is safely classed with the great men of all ages, his modest challenge seems like a condescension of the immortal President to his rival. It then seemed an act of temerity bordering on madness. Lincoln's friends thought it rash. Douglas' friends had no hope that his adversary would be so easily delivered into his hands.

Yet Lincoln was not a despised antagonist. He was the most prominent Republican in Illinois. But Douglas was the recognized head of a great national party, the giant of the Senate, the most resourceful American statesman then living. Through years of desperate battling he had successfully repelled the assaults of Seward, Sumner and Chase. He had more recently encountered with equal ease all the Southern Senators. It seemed a simple task to meet this humble Western lawyer and make his friends ashamed of their senatorial candidate. Douglas did not share the pleasant illusion of his friends. Before leaving Washington, when he heard that Lincoln was nominated, he said to Forney:

"I shall have my hands full. He is a strong man of his party,--full of wit, facts, dates,--and the best stump speaker, with his droll ways and dry jokes, in the West. He is as honest as his is shrewd; and if I beat him my victory will be hardly won."

Lincoln was burning with jealousy. He believed himself to be Douglas' full equal in mental endowment. Fortune, he thought, with a tinge of bitterness, had dealt with them most unequally, clothing his rival with the glory of a world-renowned statesman, and leaving him to waste his powers on the obscure quarrels of litigious clients in a small town. He yearned for the opportunity to measure himself with the great Senator on a conspicuous stage.

This series of debates was a rare piece of strategy on Lincoln's part. Douglas had so long been wrapped in his senatorial toga that his greatness had become exaggerated to the popular mind of Illinois; while Lincoln had been a plain, modest lawyer, moving among the people in the daily round of routine life. The dogmatic statement of the great Senator carried more weight than the profoundest argument of the clearest demonstration of the country lawyer. But these debates brought them to a common level. They measured their intellectual strength in the presence of the people, with all official trappings laid aside; and while no one could well be disappointed in Douglas' strength, the whole country was amazed at the unexpected power of Lincoln.

There were disadvantages to Douglas in this mode of combat. He must sacrifice the glamour of senatorial dignity and enter the arena on equal footing with his antagonist. He was a brilliant debater. "In the whole field of American politics no man has equaled him in the expedients and strategy of debate. * * * He was tireless, ubiquitous, unseizable. It would have been as easy to hold a globule of mercury under the finger's tip as to fasten him to a point he desired to evade. * * * In spirit he was alert, combative, aggressive; in manner patronizing and arrogant by turns." But he had to meet in argument a man of imperturbably temper, who had thought deeply on the great questions of the time, who by unerring instinct could lay his finger on every flaw in his chain of reasoning, could rise to heights of eloquence beyond the reach of his unimaginative mind and pour out streams of quaint humor that must have filled him with despair.

So great was the interest of the people in this extraordinary contest that it was found impossible to hold the meetings in halls. They were held during the warm autumn days in the open air, where the crowds, numbering from five to twenty thousand, struggled to get within range of the speakers' voices.

It would be difficult to conceive a more picturesque contest than that now waged by these politicians as they strove for the mastery, and the enormous crowds of friends and sympathizers listened with intense interest to the weighty arguments, or shouted applause when their favorite scored a point. The audiences, consisting largely of farmers, who had made long journeys in wagons and lived in tents or camped out in the open air while awaiting the great event, were in stern earnest, despite their holiday appearance, and listened with thoughtful faces and troubled hearts as the grave theme was discussed which had distracted the country for years.

And the orators, who were unconsciously playing a great role on the historic stage, were surely among the most interesting products of modern times. Lincoln's lank, ungainly figure, nearly six and a half feet tall, clad in loose fitting clothes, contrasted oddly with the short, stout figure of Douglas, barely five feet in height, trimly and rather sprucely dressed. The sad, calm face o Lincoln, his humble and unheroic bearing, were in marked contrast with the finely chiseled, powerful, defiant face and magnificent Napoleonic head surmounting the short, thick neck of Douglas, who strode with kingly air before he admiring throngs. The manner of Douglas was so masterful and strong that a wavering audience must have been swept away by it. His finely modulated voice reached with ease to the utmost limits of the crowds as he thundered out his decisive arguments or condescended to compliment his aspiring rival; while Lincoln manifestly labored to so pitch his unmusical voice that the distant listeners could hear, and was never betrayed into a single gracious compliment to the distinguished Senator whose seat he aspired to fill. And the contestants, however great their posthumous fame, were as yet merely ambitious politicians, supremely interested in winning the splendid prize. To Lincoln the possibility of a seat in the Senate was stimulus enough. Douglas was in mid career, assured of the Presidency in the near future, but compelled at all hazards to hold the ground already won. His commanding eminence attracted universal attention to the contest. He must not only win, but bear himself throughout with the air of an assured conqueror.

With all their disparity of rank and fame, they were not badly matched, and all the substantial advantages of the situation lay with Lincoln. The greatness of Douglas' fame excited sympathy for his rival. Success in the contest would give power and prestige to Lincoln, and even defeat would not be humiliating. Douglas could not expect much glory even from victory. Though he crushed his opponent in argument, he must still measure himself with the Douglas of the Senate and not fall below his own standard. In his contest for the Senate, he must remember the Presidency and shape his arguments for a larger audience than that addressed by Lincoln.

During the period of the debates both were actively engaged in the State campaign, addressing one or two audiences daily, so arranging their routes as to meet at the appointed times and places. On August 21st, in presence of a vast multitude, Douglas opened the first debate at Ottawa.

"Prior to 1854," he said, "this country was divided into two great political parties, known as the Whig and Democratic parties. Both were national and patriotic. * * * Whig principles had no boundary sectional line, * * * but applied and were proclaimed wherever the Constitution ruled or the American flag waved over American soil. So it was, and so it is, with the great Democratic party, which from the days of Jefferson to this period has proven itself to be the historic party of this Nation. * * * The Whig party and the Democratic party jointly adopted the Compromise measures of 1850 as the basis of a proper and just solution of this slavery question in all its forms. Clay was the great leader, with Webster on his right and Cass on his left, and sustained by the patriots in the Whig and Democratic ranks. * * * * In 1851 the Whig party and the Democratic party united in Illinois in approving the principles of the Compromise measures of 1850. * * * In 1852 the Whig party in Convention at Baltimore declared the Compromise measures of 1850 a suitable adjustment of that question. * * * * The Democratic Convention assembled in Baltimore the same year and adopted the Compromise measures of 1850 as the basis of Democratic action. * * * They both stood on the same platform with regard to the slavery question. That platform was the right of the people of each State and Territory to decide their local and domestic institutions for themselves, subject only to the Federal Constitution.

"In 1854 I introduced into the Senate a bill to organize the Territories of Kansas and Nebraska on that principle which had been adopted in the Compromise measures of 1850, and indorsed by the Whig party and the Democratic party in National Convention in 1852. * * * Thus you see that up to 1854, when the Kansas-Nebraska bill was brought into Congress for the purpose of carrying out the principles which both parties up to that time had indorsed and approved, there was no division of opinion in this country in regard to that principle, except the opposition of the Abolitionists. In the House of Representatives of Illinois upon a resolution asserting that principle every Whig and every Democrat voted in the affirmative."

In 1854 Lincoln, the leader of the Whigs, and Trumbull, one of the Democratic chiefs, entered into an arrangement to dissolve the old Whig and Democratic parties and to unite the members of both into the Abolition party under the name and guise of a Republican party. The terms were that Lincoln should have Shield's place in the Senate, then about to become vacant, and that Trumbull should have Douglas' seat when his term expired. Lincoln went to work to Abolitionize the old Whig party, pretending that he was as good a Whig as ever, and Trumbull began preaching Abolitionism in milder and lighter form, hoping to Abolitionize the Democratic party. The party met at Springfield in October, 1854, and proclaimed its platform. This document christened the coalition the Republican party. It pledged the party to bring the administration of the Government back to the control of first principles; to restore Kansas and Nebraska to the position of free Territories; to repeal the Fugitive Slave Law; to restrict slavery to those States in which it existed; to prohibit the admission of any more slave States into the Union; to abolish slavery in the District of Columbia; to exclude it from all the Territories and resist the acquirement of more unless it should be prohibited therein. He asked Lincoln to answer whether he stood pledged to each article in that creed and would carry it out.

"I ask Abraham Lincoln to answer these questions in order that when I trot him down to lower Egypt (Southern Illinois) I may put the same questions to him. My principles are the same everywhere. I can proclaim them alike in the North and the South, the East and the West. My principles will apply wherever the Constitution prevails and the American flag waves. I desire to know whether Mr. Lincoln's principles will bear transplanting from Ottawa to Jonesboro. I put these questions to him to-day distinctly and ask an answer. I have a right to an answer, for I quote from the platform of the Republican party, made by himself and others at the time that party was formed and bargain made by Lincoln to dissolve and kill the old Whig party and transfer its members, bound hand and foot to the Abolition party. * * * I mean nothing personally disrespectful or unkind to Lincoln. I have known him for nearly twenty-five years. There were many points of sympathy between us when we first got acquainted. We were both comparatively boys and both struggling with poverty in a strange land. I was a school teacher in the town of Winchester, and he a flourishing grocery keeper in the town of Salem. * * * I made as good a school teacher as I could and, when a cabinet maker, I made a good bedstead and tables, although my old boss said I succeeded better with bureaus and secretaries than anything else. * * * Lincoln was then just as good at telling an anecdote as now. He could beat any of the boys wrestling or running a foot race, in pitching quoits or tossing a copper, could ruin more liquor than all the boys of the town together, and the dignity and impartiality with which he presided at a horse race or a fist fight excited the admiration and won the praise of everybody."

After Lincoln and Trumbull had formed their combination to Abolitionize the old parties and put themselves into the Senate, he said, Trumbull broke faith by demanding Shield's place for himself when it fell vacant and leaving Lincoln to fight for Douglas' seat two years later. Trumbull was stumping the State for Lincoln in order to quiet him. Lincoln was opposed to the Dred Scott decision and would not submit to it because it deprived the negro of the rights and privileges of citizenship.

"Do you desire," he asked, "to * * * allow the free negroes to flow in and cover your prairies with black settlements? Do you desire to turn this beautiful State into a free negro colony, in order that when Missouri abolishes slavery she can send one hundred thousand emancipated slaves into Illinois to become citizens and voters on an equality with yourselves? * * * Mr. Lincoln, following the example and lead of all the little Abolition orators who go around and lecture in the basements of schools and churches, reads from the Declaration of Independence that all men were created equal, and then asks, 'How can you deprive the negro of that equality which God and the Declaration of Independence awards him?'" * * *

"Now I do not believe that the Almighty ever intended the negro to be the equal of the white man. If he did he has been a long time demonstrating the fact. For thousands of years the negro has been a race upon the earth and during all that time, in all latitudes and climates, wherever he has wandered or been taken, he has been inferior to the race which he there met. He belongs to an inferior race and must always occupy an inferior position. The question, what rights and privileges shall be conferred on the negro, is one which each State and Territory must decide for itself. This doctrine of Mr. Lincoln, of uniformity among the institutions of the different States, is a new doctrine, never dreamed of by Washington, Madison or the founders of this Government. Mr. Lincoln and the Republican party set themselves up as wiser than these men who made this Government which has flourished for seventy years under the principle of popular sovereignty, recognizing the right of each state to do as it pleased. Under that principle we have grown from a nation of three or four millions to a nation of about thirty millions of people; we have crossed the Allegheny Mountains and filled up the whole Northwest, turning the prairie into a garden and building up churches and schools, thus spreading civilization and Christianity where before there was nothing but savage barbarism.

"Under that principle we have become, from a feeble nation, the most powerful on the face of the earth; and if we only adhere to that principle, we can go forward increasing in territory, in power, in strength and in glory, until the Republic of America shall be the North Star that shall guide the friends of freedom throughout the civilized world. * * * I believe that this new doctrine preached by Mr. Lincoln and his party will dissolve the Union if it succeeds. They are trying to array all the Northern States in one body against the South, to excite a sectional war between the free States and the slave States, in order that the one or the other may be driven to the wall."

When the applause subsided, Lincoln rose to reply. Addressing himself first to the personal matters contained in Douglas' speech, he denied the charge of a secret bargain between himself and Trumbull dividing the two seats in the Senate between them. "All I have to say upon that subject is, that I think no man--not even Judge Douglas--can prove it, because it is not true." He denied utterly that he had anything to do with the Republican platform drafted by the party leaders in 1854, having refused to meet with the committee or take any part in the organization.

"I have no means," he said, " of totally disproving such charges as this. I cannot prove a negative; but have a right to say that, when he makes an affirmative charge, he must offer some proof of its truth. Douglas' argument about 'perfect social and political equality with the negro' is but a specious and fantastic arrangement of words by which a man can prove a horse chestnut to be a chestnut horse. I will say here, while upon the subject, that I have no purpose directly or indirectly, to interfere with the institution of slavery in the States where it exists. I believe I have no lawful right to do so. I have no purpose to introduce political and social equality between the white and black races. There is a physical difference between the two, which in my judgement will forever forbid their living together upon a footing of perfect equality; and inasmuch as it becomes a necessity that there must be a difference, I am in favor of the race to which I belong having the superior position. I agree with Judge Douglas that the negro is not my equal in many respects--certainly not in color--perhaps not in moral or intellectual endowment. But in the right to eat the bread, without the leave of anybody else, which his own hand earns, he is my equal and the equal of Judge Douglas and the equal of every living man. * * *

"In the history of our Government this institution of slavery has always been an apple of discord and an element of division in the house. I have a right to say that in regard to this question the Union is a house divided against itself. The public mind did formerly rest in the belief that slavery was in the course of ultimate extinction. But lately Douglas and those acting with him have placed it on a new basis which looks to the perpetuity and nationalization of slavery. * * * * I believe we shall not have peace upon the question until the opponents of slavery arrest the further spread of it and place it where the public mind shall rest in the belief that it is in the course of ultimate extinction; or, on the other hand, that its advocates will push it forward until it shall become alike lawful in all the States, old as well as new, North as well as South.

"Now, I believe if we could arrest the spread and place it where Washington and Jefferson and Madison paced it, it would be in the course of ultimate extinction and the public mind would, as for eighty years past, believe that it was in the course of ultimate extinction. The crisis would be passed and the institution might be let alone for a hundred years, if it should live so long, in the States where it exists; yet it would be going out of existence in the way best for both the black and the white races. * * * Popular sovereignty as now applied to the question of slavery, does allow the people of a Territory to have slavery if they want it, but does not allow them not to have it if they do not want it. * * * As I understand the Dred Scott decision, if any one man wants slaves all the rest have no way of keeping that one man from holding them. * * *

"The Nebraska bill contains this clause: 'It being the true intent and meaning of this bill not to legislate slavery into any Territory or STATE.' I have always been puzzled to know what business the word State had in that connection. Judge Douglas knows. He put it there. * * * What was it placed there for? After seeing the Dred Scott decision, which holds that the people cannot exclude slavery from a Territory, if another Dred Scott decision shall come holding that they cannot exclude it from a State, we shall discover that when the word was originally put there it was in view of something that was to come in due time, we shall see that it was the other half of something.

"I ask the attention of the people here assembled to the course that Judge Douglas is pursuing every day as bearing upon this question of making slavery national. In the first place what is necessary to make slavery national? Not war. There is no danger that the people of Kentucky will shoulder their muskets, and, with a young nigger stuck on every bayonet, march into Illinois and force them upon us. There is no danger of our going over there and making war upon them. Then what is necessary for the nationalization of slavery? It is simply the next Dred Scott decision. It is merely for the Supreme Court to decide that no State under the Constitution can exclude it, just as they have already decided that Congress nor the territorial legislature can do it. When that is decided and acquiesced in the whole thing is done. * * * Let us consider what Judge Douglas is doing every day to that end. What influence is he exerting on public sentiment? With public sentiment nothing can fail; without it nothing can succeed. Consequently, he who moulds public sentiment goes deeper than he who enacts statutes or pronounces decisions. He makes statutes possible or impossible to be executed. * * *

"Judge Douglas is a man of vast influence. Consider the attitude he occupies at the head of a large party. This man sticks to a decision which forbids the people of a Territory from excluding slavery, and he does so not because it is right in itself, but because it has been decided by the Court; and, being decided by the Court, he is, and you are, bound to take it in your political action as law. * * * You will bear in mind that thus committing himself unreservedly to this decision commits him to the next one just as firmly as to this. The next decision, as much as this, will be a 'Thus saith the Lord.' It is nothing that I point out to him that his great prototype, General Jackson, did not believe in the binding force of decisions. It is nothing to him that Jefferson did not so believe. He claims now to stand on the Cincinnati platform which affirms that Congress cannot charter a national bank, in the teeth of that old standing decision that Congress can charter a bank. And I remind him of another piece of history on the question of respect for judicial decisions belonging to a time when the large party to which Judge Douglas belongs were displeased with a decision of the Supreme Court of Illinois, because they had decided that a Governor could not remove a Secretary of State. I know that he will not deny that he was then in favor of overslaughing that decision by the mode of adding five new Judges, so as to vote down the four older ones. Not only so, but it ended in the Judge's sitting down on that very bench as one of the five new Judges to break down the four old ones.

"Now, when the Judge tells me that men appointed conditionally to sit as members of a Court will have to catechized beforehand upon some subject, I say, 'You know, Judge; you have tried it.' When he says a Court of this kind will lose the confidence of all men, will be prostituted and disgraced by such a proceeding, I say, 'You know best, Judge; you have been through the mill.' But I cannot shake Judge Douglas' teeth loose from the Dred Scott decision. Like some obstinate animal that will hang on, when he has once got his teeth fixed, you may cut off a leg, or you may tear away an arm, still he will not relax his hold. He hangs to the last to the Dred Scott decision. These things show there is a purpose strong as death and eternity for which he adheres to this decision and for which he will adhere to all other decisions of the same Court. * * * When he invites any people willing to have slavery to establish it, he is blowing out the moral lights around us. When he says he cares not whether slavery is voted down or voted up--that is the sacred right of self-government--he is, in my judgement, penetrating the human soul and eradicating the light of reason and the love of liberty. * * *

"And now I will only say that when, by all these means and appliances, he shall succeed in bringing public sentiment to an exact accordance with his own; when these vast assemblages shall echo back all these sentiments; when they shall come to repeat his views and to avow his principles and to say all that he says on these mighty questions, then it needs only the formality of a second Dred Scott decision, which he endorses in advance, to make slavery alike lawful in all the States, old as well as new, North as well as South."

Douglas, in his brief reply, reminded the audience that Lincoln had not frankly answered the question put in his opening speech; whether he approved of each article of the Republican resolutions adopted in Springfield in October, 1854. Lincoln's only answer had been that he was not present and had nothing to do with drafting the resolutions. "But this denial is a miserable quibble to avoid the main issue, which is that this Republican platform declares in favor of the unconditional repeal of the Fugitive Slave Law. His reply to all these questions is 'I was not on the Committee at the time; I was up in Tazewell County trying a case.' I put to him the question whether, if the people of the Territory, when they had sufficient population to make a State, should form their Constitution recognizing slavery, he would vote for or against its admission? He is a candidate for the United States Senate and it is possible that, if he should be elected, he would have to vote directly on that question. He dodges it also under the cover that he was not on the Committee. * * * He knows I will trot him down to Egypt. I intend to make him answer there. * * * The Convention to which I have been alluding pledges itself to exclude slavery from all the Territories. * * * I want to know whether he approves that provision. * * * I want to know whether he will resist the acquirement of any more territory, unless slavery therein shall be prohibited. These are practical questions, based upon the fundamental principles of the black Republican party; and I want to know whether he is the first, last and only choice of a party with whom he does not agree in principle.

"He does not deny but that that principle was unanimously adopted by the Republican party; and now I want to know whether that party is unanimously in favor of a man who does not adopt that creed and agree with them in their principles; I want to know whether the man who does not agree with them and who is afraid to avow his differences is the first, last and only choice of the party. * * * The party stands pledged that they will never support Lincoln until he has pledged himself to that platform; but he cannot devise his answer. He has not made up his mind whether he will or not. * * * I have not brought a charge of moral turpitude against him. When he brings one against me, instead of disproving it I will say that it is a lie and let him prove it if he can. * * *

"Mr. Lincoln has not character enough for integrity and truth merely on his own ipse dixit to arraign President Buchanan, President Pierce and nine Judges of the Supreme Court, not one of whom would be complimented by being put on an equality with him. There is an unpardonable presumption in any man putting himself up before thousands of people and pretending that his ipse dixit, without proof, without fact and without truth, is enough to bring down and destroy the purest and best of living men. * * * The word 'State' as well as 'Territory' was put into the Nebraska bill to knock in the head this Abolition doctrine that there will be no more slave States even if the people want them. * * * The people of Missouri formed a Constitution as a slave State and asked admission into the Union; but the Free Soil party of the North, being in a majority, refused to admit her because she had slavery as one of her institutions. Hence, the first slavery agitation arouse upon a State and not upon a Territory. * * * The whole Abolition agitation arose on that doctrine of prohibiting a State from coming in with slavery or not as it pleased, and that same doctrine is here in this Republican platform of 1854."

The peculiar difficult of meeting Douglas in argument before a popular audience is here exhibited in its most perfect form. The persuasive force of his last proposition lay in a most ingenious play on the words "State" and "Territory." Although the people of Missouri had formed a State Constitution, they did not become a State until Congress approved it and formally admitted them. During the entire period of dispute they continued a Territory. Douglas' argument assumes that they became a State on forming a Constitution.

Chapter XV. The Debates with Lincoln Continued.

The second debate was held at Freeport on August 27th. Lincoln opened his speech with a series of answers to the questions asked at Ottawa.

"I do not," he said, * * * "stand in favor of the unconditional repeal of the Fugitive Slave law. * * *

"I do not * * * stand pledged against the admission of any more slave States into the Union. * * * *

"I do not stand pledged against the admission of a new State. * * * with such a Constitutions as the people * * * may see fit to make. * * *

"I do not stand pledged to the abolition of slavery in the District of Columbia. * * *

"I'm impliedly, if not expressly, pledged to a belief in the right and duty of Congress to prohibit slavery in all the United States Territories. * * *

"I am not opposed to the honest acquisition of territory. * * * I would or would not oppose such acquisition accordingly as I might think such acquisition would or would not aggravate the slavery question among ourselves."

The questions asked and answered were, whether he was PLEDGED to any of these things. He was willing, however, to state what he really thought of them.

"I do not hesitate to say that * * * under the Constitution of the United States the people of the Southern States are entitled to a Congressional Fugitive Slave Law. * * * The existing Fugitive Slave Law should have been so framed as to be free from some of the objections that pertain to it without lessening its efficiency. * * * * In regard to the admission of any more slave States into the Union, I state to you frankly that I would be exceedingly sorry ever to be put in a position of having to pass upon that question. I should be exceedingly glad to know that there would never be another slave State admitted into the Union; but I must add that, if slavery be kept out of the Territories during their territorial existence, * * * * and then the people shall * * * adopt a slave Constitution, * * * I see no alternative but to admit them into the Union. * * * I should not be in favor of abolishing slavery in the District of Columbia, unless upon the condition that abolition should be gradual; that it should be on the vote of a majority of the qualified voters of the District; and that compensation be made to unwilling owners. * * * What I am saying here I suppose I say to a vast audience as strongly tending to Abolitionism as any audience in the State of Illinois, and I believe I am saying that which, if it would be offensive to any persons and render them enemies to myself, would be offensive to persons in this audience." He then asked Douglas four questions:

1st. "If the people of Kansas shall * * * adopt a State Constitution and ask admission * * * * before they have the requisite number of inhabitants under the English bill, * * * will you vote to admit them?

2nd. "Can the people of a * * * Territory in any lawful way, against the wish of any citizen, * * * exclude slavery from its limits prior to the formation of a State Constitution?

3rd. "If the Supreme Court * * * * shall decide that States cannot exclude slavery from their limits, are you in favor of acquiescing in, adopting and following such decision as a rule of political action?

4th. "Are you in favor of acquiring additional territory in disregard of how such action may affect the Nation on the slavery question?

When the Nebraska bill was introduced, he continued, it was declared the intent and meaning of the act not to legislate slavery into any State or Territory or to exclude it therefrom, but to leave the people perfectly free to regulate their own domestic institutions in their own way. Chase of Ohio introduced an amendment expressly declaring that the people of a Territory should have the power to exclude slavery if they saw fit. Douglas and those who agreed with him, voted it down. A little later the Supreme Court decided that a territorial legislature had no right to exclude slavery.

"For men who did intend that the people of the Territory should have the right to exclude slavery * * * * the voting down of Chase's amendment is wholly inexplicable. It is a puzzle, a riddle. But * * * with men who did look forward to such a decision * * * * the voting down of that amendment would be perfectly rational and intelligible. It would keep Congress from coming into collision with the decision when it was made. * * * If there was an intention or expectation that such a decision was to follow, it would not be very desirable for the Democratic Supreme Court to decide one way when the party in Congress had decided the other. Hence it would be very rational for men expecting such a decision to keep the niche in that law clear for it. * * * It looks to me as though here was the reason why Chase's amendment was voted down. * * * If it was done for a different reason, * * * he knows what that reason was and can tell us what it was. * * * It will be vastly more satisfactory to the country for him to give some other intelligible, plausible reason why it was voted down than to stand upon his dignity and call people liars."

Cass, it was said, on behalf of the Democrats in the Senate, proposed to Chase that he so change his amendment as to provide that the people of a Territory should have power either to introduce or exclude slavery, and they would accept it. Chase, having conscientious scruples on the question of slavery, declined to do this and his amendment was voted down. But it was quite possible for them to have accepted Chase's amendment, forbidden by the Senate rule, but an amendment to the amended bill, which was permitted.

Douglas, in his reply, with admirable readiness, addressed himself to Lincoln's four questions. "In reference to Kansas," he said, "it is my opinion that, as she has population enough to constitute a slave State, she has people enough for a free State. * * * The next question is, 'Can the people of a Territory * * * exclude slavery prior to the formation of a State Constitution?' * * * In my opinion they can. * * * It matters not in what way the Supreme Court may hereafter decide as to the abstract question whether slavery may or may not go into a Territory under the Constitution, the people have the lawful means to introduce it or exclude it as they please, for the reason that slavery cannot exist a day or an hour anywhere, unless it is supported by local police regulations. Those police regulations can only be established by the local legislature; and if the people are opposed to slavery they will elect representatives to that body who will, by unfriendly legislation, effectually prevent the introduction of it into their midst. If on the contrary they are for it, their legislation will favor its extension. Hence, no matter what the decision of the Supreme Court may be on that abstract question, still the right of the people to make a slave Territory or a free Territory, is perfect and complete under the Nebraska bill."

This bill provided that the legislative power of the Territory should extend to all rightful subjects of legislation. It made no exception as to slavery, but gave full power to introduce or exclude it. What more could Chase's amendment do? Chase offered it for the purpose of having it rejected. He expected it to be capital for small politicians, and he was not mistaken. He was amazed that Lincoln should ask his third question. He had denounced in the Senate an article in the Washington Union claiming that any provision in the laws or Constitutions of the free States excluding slavery was in conflict with the Constitution of the United States. Senator Toombs, on behalf of the South, had utterly repudiated the doctrine. The question cast an imputation upon the Supreme Court. Such a decision was not possible. It would be an act of moral treason that no man on the bench could ever descend to.

"As to Lincoln's fourth question," he said: "I answer, that whenever it becomes necessary in our growth and progress to acquire more territory, I am in favor of it without reference to the question of slavery; and when we have acquired it I would leave the people free to do as they please, either to make it slave or free territory as they preferred. * * * I tell you, increase, multiply and expand is the law of this Nation's existence. * * * Just as fast as our interests and our destiny require additional territory in the North, in the South or on the islands of the ocean, I am for it; and, when we acquire it, will leave the people * * * free to do as they please on the question of slavery and every other question."

At all the Republican Congressional Conventions held in Illinois in 1854, the resolutions adopted declared that the continued aggressions of slavery were destructive of the best rights of a free people and must be resisted by the united political action of all good men; Kansas and Nebraska must be made free Territories, the Fugitive Slave Law repealed, slavery restricted to the States in which it then existed, no more slave States admitted, slavery excluded from the Territories and no more Territories acquired unless slavery therein were prohibited; and no man must be supported for office unless positively pledged to support these principles.

"Yet Lincoln denies that he stands on this platform and declares that he would not like to be placed in a position where he would have to vote for these things. * * * I do not think there is much danger of his being placed in such a position. * * * I propose, out of mere kindness, to relieve him from any such necessity."

When the legislature elected in 1854 came to choose between Lincoln and

Trumbull for Senator, before a ballot was taken, Lovejoy, the Abolitionist introduced resolutions declaring that slavery must be excluded from all the territory
then owned or thereafter acquired by the United States; that no more slave States
should be admitted and that the Fugitive Slave Law should be unconditionally repealed. On the following day every man who had voted for these resolutions, with
two exceptions, voted for Lincoln. Members so voting were all pledged to vote for
no man who was not pledged to support their platform. "Either Lincoln was committed to these propositions, or your members violated their faith. Take either
horn of the dilemma you choose. There is no dodging the question; I want Lincoln's answer. He is altogether undecided on these grave questions and does not
know what to think or do. If elected Senator he will have to decide. Do not put
him in a position that would embarrass him so much. He does not know whether
he would vote for the admission of more slave States, yet he has declared his belief
that this Union cannot endure with slave States in it. I do not think that the people
of Illinois desire a man to represent them who would like to be put to the test on
the performance of a high constitutional duty.

"I will retire in shame from the Senate of the United States when I am not willing to be put to the test in the performance of my duty. I have been put to severe
tests. I have stood by my principles in fair weather and foul, in the sunshine and
in the rain. I have defended the great principles of self-government here among
you when Northern sentiment ran in a torrent against me, and I have defended that
same great principle when Southern sentiment came down like an avalanche upon
me. I was not afraid of any test they put me to. I knew my principles were right;
I knew my principles were sound; I knew that the people would see in the end hat
I had done right and I knew that the God of heaven would smile upon me if I was
faithful in the performance of my duty. * * *

At the time the Nebraska bill was introduced, Lincoln says there was a conspiracy between the Judges of the Supreme Court, President Pierce, President Buchanan and myself, that bill and the decision of the court to break down the barriers
and establish slavery all over the Union. * * *

"Mr. Buchanan was at that time in England and did not return for a year or
more after. That fact proves the charge to be false as against him. * * * The Dred
Scott case was not then before the Supreme Court at all; * * * * and the Judges in all

probability knew nothing of it. * * * * As to President Pierce, his high character as a man of integrity and honor is enough to vindicate him from such a charge; and as to myself I pronounce the charge an infamous lie whenever and wherever made and by whomsoever made."

Lincoln closed the debate. As to the discrepancy between the various Republican resolutions adopted in local conventions in 1854 and the views stated in his opening speech, he said that at the beginning of the Nebraska agitation a new era in American politics began.

"In our opposition to that measure we did not agree with one another in everything. * * * * These meetings which the Judge has alluded to and the resolutions he has read from were local. * * * We at last met together in 1856 from all parts of the State and agreed upon a common platform. * * * We agreed then upon a platform for the party throughout the entire State and now we are all bound to that platform. * * * If any one expects that I will do anything not signified by our Republican platform and my answers here to-day, I will tell you very frankly that person will be deceived. I do not ask for the vote of anyone who supposes that I have secret purposes or pledges that I dare not speak out. * * * Douglas says if I should vote for the admission of a slave State I would be voting for the dissolution of the Union, because I hold that the Union cannot permanently exist half slave and half free. * * * It does not at all follow that the admission of a single slave State will permanently fix the character and establish this as a universal slave Nation."

In March, 1856, Douglas, speaking in the Senate upon an article published, apparently by authority, in the Washington Union, the organ of the Administration, charged a conspiracy between the President, his cabinet and the Lecompton Convention to establish the proposition that all State laws and Constitutions, which prohibited the citizens of one State from settling in another with their slave property, were violations of the Constitution of the United States. He declared that a fatal blow was being struck at the sovereignty of the States. Charges of conspiracy were not entirely unheard of when the one was made at Springfield so sharply condemned by Douglas.

"But his eye is farther South now than it was last March. His hope then rested on the idea of visiting the great black Republican party and making it the tail of his new kite. He was then expected from day to day to turn Republican and place himself at the head of our organization. He has found that these despised black Republicans estimate him, by a standard which he has taught them, none to well. Hence he is crawling back into the old camp and you will find him eventually installed in full fellowship among those whom he was then battling and with whom he still pretends to be at such fearful variance."

There is an interesting and well authenticated tradition, perhaps too strongly established to be questioned, that Lincoln's second interrogatory was designed as a snare for Douglas and that he was forced by it to proclaim his unfortunate doctrine of unfriendly legislation, which gave such deep offense to the South. It is related on the highest authority that on the night before the Freeport debate, "Lincoln was catching a few hours' rest at a railroad center named Mendota, to which place the converging trains brought, after midnight, a number of excited Republican leaders on their way to attend the great meeting at the neighboring town of Freeport. * * * * Lincoln's bedroom was invaded by an improvised caucus, and the ominous question was once more brought under consideration. The whole drift of advice ran against putting the interrogatory (number two) to Douglas, but Lincoln persisted in his determination to force him to answer it. Finally his friends in a chorus cried: 'If you do, you can never be Senator.'

"'Gentlemen,' replied Lincoln, 'I am killing larger game. If Douglas answers, he can never be President, and the battle of 1860 is worth a hundred of this.'"

Whatever may be the truth as to the Mendota conference, it is unjust to Douglas to say that he was surprised by the question, or that his answer was a mere extemporized feat of ingenuity to meet an embarrassing exigency. Long before this and on many occasions he had announced his opinion that the people of a Territory could by unfriendly legislation, in defiance of the Constitution, the Supreme Court and Congress, effectually prevent slavery among themselves. It was one of his most deliberately formed, openly avowed and widely known opinions. It is incredible that Lincoln and his advisors were in doubt how he would answer the question. Whatever may be our view of the soundness of his doctrine, it is not just to the ablest debater and foremost statesman of the time to say that he was taken by surprise and driven into a corner by a question which, as he was taken by surprise and driven into a corner by a question which, as he said then, he had answered a hundred times from every stump in Illinois.

The third debate was held at Jonesboro, near the southern boundary of the State, on September 15th.

Douglas, in his opening speech, stated anew his now familiar argument that the Republican party was sectional, threatening to disrupt the Union by its slavery agitation, while the Democratic party was national, with a wholesome creed, alike applicable in all latitudes. Lincoln and Trumbull had conspired to abolitinize the old parties and secure seats in the Senate. Lincoln's doctrine of the house divided against itself was examined and the implied threat emphasized that Southern institutions must be overthrown and a dead level of uniformity reached in order that the Government should stand. The finality of the Dred Scott decision and the exclusion of negroes from the Declaration of Independence were insisted on. Much of the speech was devoted to the local and transient questions of Illinois politics.

Lincoln, replying to the charge that the slavery agitation was the result of the aggressive attitude of Northern Abolitionists, again insisted that the propagandists of slavery were the aggressors, having attempted to change it from a local and declining institution and spread it through all the Territories, removing it "from the basis on which the fathers left it to the basis of its perpetuation and nationalization." The agitation began with the repeal of the Missouri Compromise.

"Who," he asked, "did that? Why, when we had peace under the Missouri Compromise, could you not have left it alone?"

He quoted Douglas' speech in the Senate on June 9th, 1856, in which he had declared that "whether the people could exclude slavery prior to the formation of a Constitution or not, was a question to be decided by the Supreme Court. * * * * When he says, after the Supreme Court has decided the question, that the people may yet exclude slavery by any means whatever, he does virtually say that it is not a question for the Supreme Court. * * * the proposition that slavery cannot enter a new country without police regulations is historically false. * * * Slavery was originally planted upon this continent without these police regulations. * * * How came the Dred Scott decision to be made? It was made upon the case of a negro being taken and actually held in slavery in Minnesota Territory, claiming his freedom because the act of Congress prohibited his being so held there. Will the Judge pretend that Dred Scott was not held there without police regulations? * * * * This shows that there is vigor enough in slavery to plant itself in a new country, even against unfriendly legislation. It takes not only law, but the enforcement of the law, to keep it out. This is the history of this country upon the subject. *** The first thing a Senator does is swear to support the Constitution of the United States. Suppose a Senator believes, as Douglas does, that the Constitution guarantees the right to hold slaves in a Territory. How can he clear his oath unless he supports such legislation as is necessary to enable the people to enjoy their property? Can you, if you swear to support the Constitution, and believe that the Constitution establishes a right, clear your oath without giving it support? **** There can be nothing in the words, 'support the Constitution,' if you may run counter to it by refusing to support it. * *** And what I say here will hod with still more force against the Judge's doctrine of unfriendly legislation. *** Is not Congress itself bound to give legislative support to any right that is established in the United States Constitution? A Member of Congress swears to support the Constitution *** and if he sees a right established by that Constitution which needs specific legislative protection, can he clear his oath without giving that protection. *** If I acknowledge *** that this (Dred Scott) decision properly construes the Constitution, I cannot conceive that I would be less than a perjured man if I should refuse in Congress to give such protection to that property as in its nature is needed."

He then stated his fifth interrogatory: If slave-holding citizens of the United States Territory should need and demand congressional legislation for the protection of their slave property in such Territory, would you as a Member of Congress, vote for or against such legislation?

Douglas in his reply took up Lincoln's rather evasive answer to his second interrogatory submitted at Ottawa. "Lincoln," he said, "would be exceedingly sorry to be put in a position where he would have to vote on the question of the admission of slave States. Why is he a candidate for the Senate if he would be sorry to be put in that position? **** If Congress keeps out slavery by law while it is a Territory and then the people should have a fair chance and should adopt slavery, he supposes he would have to admit the State. Suppose Congress should not keep slavery out during their territorial existence, then how would he vote when the people applied for admission with a slave Constitution? That he does not answer; and that is the condition of every Territory we have now got. His answer only applies to a given case which he knows does not exist in any Territory. But Mr. Lincoln does not want to be held responsible for the black Republican doctrine of no more slave States. Why are men running for Congress in the northern Distracts and taking that Abolition platform for their guide when Mr. Lincoln does not want to be held to it down here in Egypt? His party in the northern part of the State hold to that Abolition platform, and if they do not in the south, they present the extra-ordinary spectacle of 'a house divided against itself' and hence 'cannot stand.'"

In answer to Lincoln's last question, he said: "It is a fundamental article of the Democratic creed that there should be non-interference or non-intervention of Congress with slavery in the States or Territories. The Democratic party have always stood by that great principle and I stand on that platform now. ****Lincoln himself will not answer this question. *** It is true *** (he admits) that under the decision of the Supreme Court, it is the duty of a man to vote for a slave code in the Territories. If he believed in that decision he would be a perjured man if he did not give the vote. I want to know whether he is not bound to a decision which is contrary to his opinions just as much as to one in accordance with his opinions? *** Is every man in this land allowed to resist decisions he does not like and only support those which meet his approval? ****It is the fundamental principle of the judiciary that its decisions are final. ****My doctrine is that, even taking Mr. Lincoln's view that the decision recognizes the right of a man to carry his slaves into the Territories, yet after he gets them there he needs affirmative law to make that right of any value. The same doctrine applies to all other kinds of property.

"Suppose one of your merchants should move to Kansas and open a liquor store; he has a right to take groceries or liquor there; but the circumstances under which they shall be sold and all the remedies must be prescribed by local legislation; and if that is unfriendly it will drive him out just as effectually as if there was a constitutional provision against the sale of liquor. Hence, I assert, that under the Dred Scott decision you cannot maintain slavery a day in a Territory where there is an unwilling people and unfriendly legislation. If the people want slavery they will have it, and if they do not want it you cannot force it upon them."

Neither Lincoln nor Douglas could as yet fairly and fearlessly grapple with the great problem. Lincoln's virtual rejection and defiance of the decision of the Supreme Court suggests not reform but revolution. These dark hints that the decisions of the highest tribunal should not be accepted or obeyed, that they were binding only on those who believed in them, portended nothing less than war. Slavery being an established institution, recognized by the Constitution and regulated by law, had the right to exist. Lincoln and his party abhorred it and resented the injustice of the law. Obeying the dominant instinct of the race, the scrupulously observed the form of the law while waging war upon it. On the other hand it is impossible to find either legal or philosophical foundation for Douglas' arguments. Slavery had been adjudged lawful in all the Territories. The proposition gravely argued by him, that the people could lawfully exclude a thing from a place where it had a lawful right to be, was monstrous. He sternly rebuked Lincoln for his irreverence in refusing to cordially accept the Dred Scott decision and in the next breath, with shocking inconsistency, dissolved its entire force in the menstruum of unfriendly legislation. The decision was utterly repugnant to the people of the State. The both viewed it as a political rather than a philosophic problem. Both rejected it and the consequences flowing from it. Lincoln quibbled when asked to accept it as a rule governing his political conduct. Douglas, by a cunning device, sought to destroy its force as a rule of private right. Lincoln insisted on the essential dishonesty of the juggling trick by which Douglas got rid of the adjudicated law. Douglas insisted on the anarchic spirit with which Lincoln bade defiance to it.

It would be tedious to follow the debates through in detail. Necessarily the later arguments were mainly a repetition of those made in the earlier speeches. Thee was a marked falling off in the good temper and mutual courtesy of the combatants in the later stages of the contest. The abiding question to which the argument constantly recurred was that of negro slavery, as to which Lincoln was darkly oracular and Douglas was resolutely evasive. Lincoln again and again pressed Douglas to say whether he regarded slavery as wrong. Douglas persistently declined the question on the pleat that it was one wholly foreign to national politics. Each State had a right to decide for itself; and that right had been delegated to the Territories by the Compromise act of 1850 and again by the Kansas-Nebraska act of 1854.

"I look forward," he said, "to a time when each State shall be allowed to do as it pleases. If it chooses to keep slavery forever, it is not my business, but its own; if it chooses to abolish slavery, it is its own business, not mine. I care more for the great principle of self-government, the right of the people to rule, then I do for all the negroes in Christendom. I would not endanger the perpetuity of this Union, I would not blot out the great inalienable rights of the white man, for all the negroes that ever existed."

Lincoln persistently pressed his argument: "When Douglas says he don't care whether slaver is voted up or voted down, he can thus argue logically if he don't see anything wrong in it; but he cannot say so logically if he admits that slavery is wrong. He cannot say that the would as soon see a wrong voted up as voted down. When he says that slave property and horse and hog property are alike to be allowed to go into the Territories upon the principle of equality, he is reasoning truly if there is no difference between them and property; but if the one is property held rightfully and the other is wrong, then there is no equality between the right and the wrong. * * * That is the real issue. That is the issue that will continue in this country when these poor tongues of Judge Douglas and myself shall be silent. It is the eternal struggle between these two principles that have stood face to face from the beginning of time and will ever continue to struggle. The one is the common right of humanity and the other the divine right of kings. It is the same principle in whatever shape it develops. It is the same spirit that says, 'you work and toil and earn bread, and I'll eat it.' No matter in what shape it comes, whether from the mouth of a king who seeks to bestride the people of his own nation and live by the fruit of their labor or from one race of men as an apology for enslaving another race, it is the same tyrannical principle."

In the Quincy debate, and again in the last debate at Alton, Douglas, with great skill, took up the attack made upon him by the Buchanan Administration because of his alleged heresies on the Kansas question. The Washington Union in an editorial had condemned his Freeport declaration that the people could by their unfriendly attitude exclude slavery from a Territory. It argued that his plan was to exclude it by means of his device of popular sovereignty and declared that he was not a sound Democrat and had not been since 1850. He quoted from Buchanan's letter accepting the nomination, in which he warmly applauded those "principles as ancient as free government itself * * * in accordance with which * * * * the people of a Territory, like those of a State, shall decide for themselves whether slavery shall or shall not exist within their limits."

He also quoted in vindication of the soundness of his Democracy a speech of Jefferson Davis declaring that, if the inhabitants of a Territory should refuse to enact laws to protect and encourage slavery, the insecurity would be so great that the owner could not hold his slaves.

"Therefore," said Davis, "though the right would remain, the remedy being withheld, it would follow that the owner would be practically debarred from taking slave property into a Territory when the sense of its inhabitants was opposed to its introduction."

These latter arguments were addressed to the Administration Democrats, who, however, proved a quite unimportant factor in the campaign. They were an utter negation politically. Were it an academic problem, much could be said in their defense. In a time of stormy passion, they were passionless. In a time of fanatical convictions and intolerant opinions, they were coldly neutral, appealing with impotent pride to the traditions and precedents of the past.

The election was held on the 2nd of November. The Republicans elected their State ticket by a popularity of nearly 4,000, but lost the legislature. When that body met Douglas was again chose Senator.

Chapter XVI. The South Rejects Popular Sovereignty.

Although victorious in the greatest battle of his life the position of Douglas was not easy. The people of Illinois were evidently no longer in sympathy with him. The Buchanan Administration and the Southern extremists had openly declared war on him for his cool indifference to the special interests of the South, his carelessness whether slavery was voted up or voted down in the Territories, and his hostility to their plans for planting it in Kansas. He was preparing for his last struggle for the Presidency. Having won this doubtful victory at home, he decided to make a tour of the South in the hope of stimulating its waning enthusiasm. In order to hold the Senatorship it had been necessary to please Illinois, even though the South were alienated. In order to win the Presidency he now resolved to satisfy the South, even though he offended Illinois. Moreover, being at war with the Administration, he hoped to return to Washington with the prestige of a re-election and a great Southern ovation. He intended to force Buchanan and his Cabinet to sue for peace. He was political strategist enough to understand the importance of a bold front and an imposing display of power at the outset of his next campaign.

He took boat at St. Louis for New Orleans and enjoyed the leisurely autumn trip down the River. He spoke at Memphis on November 29th, and at New Orleans on December 6th. He sailed to Havana and thence to New York, where he received a royal welcome. On reaching Philadelphia he was formally welcomed at Independence Hall. He then went to Baltimore and spoke in Monument Square on the evening of January 5th, returning to Washington next day. On the 10th he resumed his seat in the Senate.

He had told the people of Illinois that, in spite of the Constitution, the Supreme Court, the President and Congress, it was within the power of the inhabitants of a

Territory to prohibit slavery by their unfriendly attitude. This doctrine was utterly abhorrent to the South, which now rested its entire case on the judicial interpretation of the Constitution and regarded all attempts to evade the full force of the Dred Scott decision as little less than treason. The net result of the struggles of a decade had been the establishment of a principle that the Constitution carried slavery with it wherever it went. To lightly treat the Constitution as a thing that could be quietly defied and annulled by the squatters, was to strip their great victory of all value and snatch from them the fruit of their labors. Had this doctrine of local nullification been sound, it was not to be expected that it would be received with enthusiasm or even with patience by men whose dearest hopes it must obviously defeat and whose subtle art and long protracted labors it utterly thwarted. But that daring sophism which attacked the very foundation of all legal authority, did violence to every sound principle of philosophy, and was utterly subversive of the peculiar and cherished doctrines of the South, should have been resorted to by Douglas to avoid defeat in Illinois, was viewed as a shameless outrage. It was believed that he had sacrificed their sacred cause in order to avoid a local reverse; that his seat in the Senate was dearer to him than their most valued interests.

It was probable that in his eagerness to win the Illinois campaign he had not considered seriously the irreconcilable repugnance of his distinctive dogma to the compact body of Southern political philosophy. It was now necessary to present it to the South in such dress that it might, if possible, gain acceptance, at least that it might not shock the deepest prejudices of that section.

In addressing his Southern audiences he attempted to take the sting out of his obnoxious doctrine by showing that it was entirely harmless. The people of the Territories, he said, doubtless had the practical power, in spite of the Constitution, statutes and decisions, to exclude slavery by their unfriendly attitude toward it. But what would determine their attitude? Clearly their selfish interests. If slavery would be profitable, their attitude would be friendly and it would take root and flourish under the protection of the law. If by reason of soil or climate it would be unprofitable, their attitude would be unfriendly and neither laws nor Constitutions could successfully foster it. But it could not injure the South to exclude slavery from regions where it could only be maintained at a loss. It was not a question of ethics, but purely of physical geography. Where soil and climate rendered it profitable, it would spring up in precisely the same way as pine trees or maize.

But it was clear to his keen eye that these feats of ingenuity were taken at their real worth. While the people treated him with gracious courtesy, they prudently reserved their judgement. They paid generous honor to the great leader whom they would gladly use but dared not trust. He had chosen to hold Illinois and had lost the South.

While he was vainly trying to woo back the alienated South, a significant event occurred in Washington. When the Senate was organized during his absence, he was removed from the chairmanship of the Committee on Territories, which he had held since his first election. This was done by the Democratic caucus and indicated a deeper resentment than he had suspected. The Puritans of Illinois had once risen in insurrection against him. The Cavaliers of the South were now sternly protesting against his easy political morals.

For six weeks he preserved almost complete silence. His situation was anomalous. The quarrel with the Administration was implacable. A few months before, the Republicans were inclined to court him; but the desperate battle with Lincoln had made it clear that his quarrel with them was on perennial questions of principle. Solitary and out of touch with all parties, he was yet recognized as the chief of the Northern Democrats and a formidable candidate for the Presidency.

While diplomatically awaiting developments, he was suddenly drawn into an important debate. On February 23rd Senator Brown of Mississippi discussed with great plainness his attitude on the slavery question. With ill concealed contempt for men whose opinions shaped themselves to suit the demands of political strategy he said:

"I at least am no spoilsman. I would rather settle one sound principle in a presidential contest than secure all the patronage of all the Presidents who have ever been elected to or retired from the office. * * * The Constitution never gave us rights and denied us the means of protecting and defending those rights. The Supreme Court has decided that we have a right to carry our slaves into the Territories and, necessarily, to have them protected after we get there. * * * I neither want to cheat nor to be cheated in the great contest that is to come off in 1860. * * * I think I understand the position of the Senator from Illinois and I dissent from it. * * * He thinks that a territorial legislature may, by non-action or unfriendly action, rightfully exclude slavery. I do not think so. * * * * The Senator from Illinois thinks the territorial legislature has the right, by non-action or by unfriendly action to exclude us with our slaves. * * * We have a right of protection for our slave property in the Territories. The Constitution as expounded by the Supreme Court awards it. We demand it, and we mean to have it."

Douglas at once answered. He said that his obnoxious doctrine only meant that the territorial legislature by the exercise of the taxing power and other functions within the limits of the Constitution could adopt unfriendly legislation which would practically drive slavery out. The real demand of the South was for a congressional slave code for the Territories. But no Northern man, whether Democrat or Republican, would ever vote for such a code. The inhabitants would protect slavery if they wanted it, if the climate were such that they could not cultivate the soil without it. It was a question of climate, of production, of self-interest, and not of constitutional law. The slave owner had no higher rights than the owner of liquor or inferior cattle, which the territorial legislature could exclude. Under the doctrine of the Kansas-Nebraska act the Territories had the right to pass such laws as they pleased, subject only to the Constitution.

If their laws conflicted with that it was the business, not of Congress, but of the Courts to decide their nullity. When Buchanan accepted the nomination in 1856, he declared that the people of a Territory, like those of a State, should decide for themselves whether slavery should exist within its limits. He could not have carried half the Democratic vote in any free State if the people had not so understood him. "I intend to use language," he continued, "which can be repeated in Chicago as well as in New Orleans, in Charleston as well as in Boston. * * * No political creed is sound or safe which cannot be proclaimed in the same sense wherever the American Flag waves over American soil. If the North and the South cannot come to a common ground on the slavery question the sooner we know it the better. * * * I tell you, gentlemen of the South, in all candor, I do not believe a Democratic candidate can ever carry one Democratic State of the North on the platform that it is the duty of the Federal Government to force the people of a Territory to have slavery when they do not want it."

Davis, the leader of the Southern Democracy, answered him. He reminded the Senate that Congress had no power to exclude slavery from a Territory and the legislature had no power except that given it by Congress. Hence it could not possibly have the power to exclude it. Douglas could not claim more than this unless he could illustrate the philosophical problem of getting more out of a tub than it contained. Congress, having no power to prohibit slavery, was bound to see that it was fully enjoyed.

"I agree with my colleague," he continued, "that we are not, with our eyes open, to be cheated, and that we have no more respect for that man who seeks to evade the performance of a constitutional duty than for one who openly wars upon constitutional rights."

Mason, of Virginia, insisted that the Constitution construed by the Supreme Court denied Congress the power to exclude slavery form a Territory. Douglas admitted that the legislature derived all its power from Congress. Hence, he must admit that it had no power to interfere with slavery.

Green, of Missouri, the new chairman of the Committee on Territories, next attacked him. Slaves, he declared, were property, as decided by the Supreme Court. The Territories of Kansas and Nebraska could not, by either direct or indirect legislation, prohibit or abolish slavery; and if they should undertake to do either it would be the duty of Congress to interpose. The legislature had no more power, by direct or indirect means to prohibit the introduction of slaves than the introduction of horses or mules, and it was a dishonest subterfuge to say that it could be done.

"What is meant by unfriendly legislation? I had thought that rights of person and property were beyond the power of legislation. * * * There never was a legislative body in existence on the face of the globe that could justly take any right of person or property from a citizen without rendering a just compensation." He reminded the Senators that in 1857 Douglas had urged the interposition of Congress in Utah affairs, even to the extent of repealing the organic act, thus recognizing that Territories were mere dependencies of the Federal Government. Why this tenderness about Kansas? A Territory had no power except what was conferred by Congress. Douglas said that all legislative power not inconsistent with the Constitution, was conferred. But if the power to destroy any kind of property was conferred, it would be consistent with the Constitution and the grant would be void. If all power not inconsistent with the Constitution was conferred by the organic act, then the power to call the Lecompton Convention and draft a Constitution was conferred.

"All the power the Territory has is derived from Congress and can be resumed at pleasure. The creature can never be equal to its creator."

Douglas said, that if the people of a Territory wanted slavery they would protect it. But suppose the majority did not want it? The Constitution still declared slaves to be property and forbade the majority to take away the property in a slave from a single individual. If they had no right to take it away, what right had they by unfriendly legislation to render it valueless? If a Territory persistently attempted to destroy a species of property protected by the Constitution, ought not Congress to intervene for the protection of the citizens?

Douglas replied to these deadly attacks. He reminded them that when they repealed the Missouri Compromise they had agreed to leave all these questions to the people of the Territories and the decision of the Supreme Court. This was the true Democratic doctrine. Davis and Mason had both said that no man holding his views could receive the support of the South for the Presidency. Yet this was the doctrine of Cass when candidate for President, but the whole South gave him their votes. When did this change of creed occur?

Davis answered briefly, regretting that Douglas had not denied or explained any of his Illinois speeches, and said he was now satisfied that he was as full of heresy as he once was of the true theory of popular sovereignty. He declared that this doctrine was "offensive to every idea of conservatism and sound government; a thing offensive to every idea of the supremacy of the laws of the United States," and announced plainly that the South would not support him for President. He persistently pressed him to say whether he meant to abide by the Dred Scott decision.

The Court, answered Douglas, had decided that neither Congress nor the territorial legislature could prohibit the settler from bringing his slaves to a Territory. "In other words, the right of transit is clear, the right of entry is clear. * * * You have the same right to hold them as other property, subject to such local laws as the legislature may constitutionally enact. If those laws render it impracticable to HOLD your property, whether it be your horse or your slave, why, it is your misfortune."

He had reached the brink of the abyss. The South was preparing for treason and rebellion. Its mood was altogether too tragic to be even amused by his philosophic refinements. It rejected them now, not with contempt, but with horror. The North, too, was in stern mood. Its abhorrence of slavery had intensified with constant agitation. It was grimly earnest in its resolve to resist all further extension of it and resented the indifference of the statesman who did not care whether the burning crime of the ages was voted up or voted down.

Douglas, who regarded the ethics of this question with indifference and who supremely desired to conciliate the South without alienating the North, blundered in plunging into this debate. The Southern Senators were unanswerably right. Since the Dred Scott decision his position was so clearly untenable that to insist upon it amid conditions so threatening seemed to them the most intolerable trifling. The Republicans looked on as pleased spectators while the battle raged between Northern and Southern Democrats and the party was hopelessly torn asunder. It was clear the part of prudence to restrain his impulsive pugnacity for the remaining weeks of the session. But when challenged to defend himself his impatient eagerness to speak was uncontrollable.

Chapter XVII. Seeking Reconciliation.

After the adjournment he devoted himself to a new and unfamiliar task. He prepared an article for Harper's Magazine on the slavery question and its relation to party politics, in which he defended his position, explained his philosophy and sought to throw light on this confused subject. The article made some stir at the time. It contained nothing, however, which he had not already said much better in his speeches. He was not a man of literary culture or habits. His thought was brightest and his eloquence highest when the battle was raging.

The article had the good fortune to provoke a rather elaborate anonymous reply from Jeremiah S. Black, Buchanan's Attorney-general. Black was a profound lawyer and better writer than Douglas. While he would have been no match for him in senatorial debate or on the stump, he completely eclipsed him as a literary controversialist. Moreover, Black was standing on firm ground, simply insisting that his party accept the decision of the Supreme Court as law and conform its conduct to it without evasion or pettifoggery; while Douglas was striving to stand in mid-air, nullifying the decision by clever tricks and condemning as anarchists the Republicans, who frankly confessed their hostility to it. He gravely argued that Congress could grant to a territorial legislature power which the Constitution denied to itself. Black's answer was crushing and showed conclusively that there was no basis in either law or logic for those peculiar doctrines in which Douglas differed from his party. Black judiciously avoided all discussion of the ethics of the question, confining himself to an examination of the legal basis of Douglas' special creed, proving clearly that it had been utterly swept away.

On the night of October 16th occurred John Brown's mad exploit at Harper's Ferry. Congress opened on December 5th. On the 12th of January Douglas' heretical opinions on the right of the people to exclude slavery from the Territories were called in question. The Southern Senators pressed upon him the fact that he had agreed to abide by the decision of the Supreme Court on the disputed question, and, now that the South had been sustained by the decision, he had virtually repudiated it by his Illinois speeches. No man holding such opinions, they declared, was a sound Democrat or could possibly receive the vote of a Southern State at the Charleston Convention. They justified their action in removing him from his chairmanship of the Committee on Territories by a rehearsal of his heretical opinions and announced their purpose to oppose his presidential aspirations. He defended himself against this irregular attack with great ability and courage, maintaining the soundness of his Democracy and imputing heresy to his accusers, who were seeking to debauch the ancient Democratic faith by infusing into it their late-invented doctrines. At last, wearied by the irregular debate, he sarcastically proposed that, as his health was poor, they all make their attacks upon him and present their charges; when they were through he would "fire at the lump" and vindicate every word he had said.

A few days later he offered a resolution to instruct the Judiciary Committee to prepare a bill to suppress and punish conspiracies in one State to invade or otherwise molest the people or property of another, and addressed the Senate upon it. He expressed his firm and deliberate conviction that the John Brown raid at Harper's Ferry was the natural, logical, inevitable result of the doctrines and teachings of the Republican party as explained and the enforced in speeches of its leaders in and out of Congress. He said that when he returned home in 1858 for the purpose of canvassing Illinois with a view to reelection, he had to meet this issue of the irrepressible conflict. Lincoln had already proclaimed the existence of inexpiable hostility between free States and slave States. Later, Seward had announced it in his Rochester speech. It was evidently the creed of his party. The Harper's Ferry outrage was a natural and logical consequence of these pernicious doctrines. John Brown was simply practicing their philosophy at Harper's Ferry. The causes that produced this invasion were still in active operation. These teachers of rebellion were disseminating their deadly principles. Let Congress pass appropriate laws and make such example of the leaders of these conspiracies as to strike terror into the hearts of the others and there would be an end of this crusade.

With all his courage in meeting recent attacks, it was plain that his only hope of the Presidency lay in the prospect of his reconciliation with the Southern leaders. They needed his help to prevent the Radicals, Seward, Chase and Lincoln, from carrying the next election. He needed their help to compass the nomination. He decided without lowering his standard to win them back by the mere efficiency of his service. But the Southern leaders were not in search of a Northern master. They wanted servants in the high places of Government not less humble than the blacks who tilled their plantations. They instinctively knew that he was not and could not be such a servant. Rather than support him they would see Seward elected. He at least frankly avowed his hostility. If they elected Douglas and he declined to obey, their position would be awkward. If a sectional Republican were elected, they could secede and set up an independent Government.

On the 7th of May Davis spoke in support of a series of radical resolutions introduced by him on February 2nd, declaring that neither Congress nor a territorial legislature had power to impair the Constitutional right of any citizen of the United States to take his slave property into the common Territories and there hold it; that it was the duty of Congress to protect this right; and that the inhabitants had no power either by direct legislation or by their unfriendly attitude to exclude slavery until they formed a State Constitution. He spoke with great force in support of them. He ascribe the authorship of the pernicious heresy of squatter sovereignty to Cass, and threw doubt on the soundness of Douglas' Democracy by a long recital of what he regarded as unsound and heretical opinions and votes. He showed the complete failure of his distinctive policy in Kansas and the authoritative rejection of his principles by the Supreme Court. While the speech was courteous and dignified in manner, apparently delivered to elucidate the subject rather than to injure Douglas, it portrayed the wreck of his statesmanship and exposed the unsoundness of his Democracy with dangerous clearness while his candidacy was in the hands of the National Convention.

A week later he replied. Already the Charleston Convention, and with it his candidacy, had virtually gone to pieces because of Southern hostility to him and his principles. Davis was the head o the Southern junta, and the debate in the Senate was known to express in cold phrase, the passions that had rent the Convention and threatened to disrupt the party.

As Douglas, anxious but unfaltering, rose to speak, there was a hush in the crowded Chamber. After a sneering allusion to his controversy with Black, he announced his purpose to defend himself against the attack made by Davis. The speech occupied two days in its delivery and was a unique and artistic piece of senatorial politics. It was addressed less to the Senate than to the adjourned Charleston Convention. He exhaustively proved the soundness of Democracy and repelled the charge of heresy by rehearsing the history of Democratic Conventions and platforms since 1848, quoting the declarations of the party and its leaders in Convention, on the platform and through the press.

Cass, he said, the author of the now deadly doctrine of popular sovereignty, was nominated in 1848. The Compromise of 1850 embodied that principle. The Kansas-Nebraska struggle was settled by expressly adopting it. The Cincinnati platform, on which all Democrats had stood for four years, distinctly affirmed it. The Charleston Convention, within a few days, had reaffirmed it. His own speeches showed that he had adhered to it constantly from the beginning of his career. The change was not in him but in the Southern wing of the party. He protested that he did not desire the nomination and only permitted his name to be used that he might be vindicated against the presumptuous efforts of a little coterie to cast doubt upon his Democracy and their attempt to proscribe him as a heretic might be rebuked.

The most hostile critic must feel some sympathy for him in his new and indefensible position. His now heretical opinions had but recently borne the authentic stamp of Democracy. His party, following its real sentiments and the judicial interpretation of the Constitution, had silently abandoned its old creed to which he still clung with tenacity and ardor.

Davis, answering, asked him the blunt question, whether, if elected President, he would sign a bill to protect slave property in States, Territories, or the District of Columbia. He declined to answer suggesting the impropriety of declaring in advance what he would do if elected.

Congress adjourned on June 25th.

Chapter XVIII. A Noontide Eclipse.

While events in Washington in the spring of 1860 were full of historic interest, greater and more memorable events were occurring in Charleston. The Democratic Convention met in that city on April 23rd, which brought to the surface a state of feeling at the South that had long been suspected but not certainly known.

There was but one prominent candidate in the field. Douglas was incomparably the most eminent Democratic statesman of the time. According to the settled custom of the party, the South, which did not ask the Presidency itself, should have supported him. But the Southern delegates had resolved that in no event should he be nominated on any platform.

He had a clear majority of the Convention. But the Democrats, though still wearing a common badge, now constituted two distinct and antagonistic parties, held together not so much by common beliefs as by habits, traditions and sentimental attachment to an old and venerable name. The Northern Democrats were wholly estranged from those of the South. The two sections of the party quarreled about the platform; yet the Southerners cared little about that matter if they could name the candidate. They did not demand a Southern man, for he could not be elected. They wanted a "Northern man with Southern principles," like Pierce or Buchanan. Of all living men the dexterous and domineering Douglas least suited their demands. He was probably the only man who could have carried a large enough Northern vote to be elected. But they could not forget that his popularity at the North was, in part, the result of his great battle against the South which had caused their disastrous defeat.

The Northern delegates insisted on merely approving the Cincinnati platform, while the Southern delegates, who hoped to render Douglas' candidacy impossible, insisted on radical pro-slavery declarations and a denial of all right of the people of a Territory to prevent the holding of slaves. After a fierce struggle the Northern platform was adopted by a small majority. Immediately the delegates from Alabama, Mississippi, South Carolina, Louisiana, Florida, Texas, Arkansas and three-fourths of that from Georgia refused to abide by it and withdrew.

The seceders organized another Convention, adopted the radical platform which had been rejected and adjourned to meet at Richmond on the 11th of June.

The regular Convention, meanwhile, found itself unable to do anything. The settled rule required a vote of two-thirds of all the delegates to select a candidate. The chairman ruled that in order to be nominated Douglas must have two-thirds of all the delegates elected, notwithstanding the secession. This required 202 votes. He had but 152 and the other 50 were not to be had. On May 3rd, after 57 ballots, the Convention adjourned to meet at Baltimore on June 18th. Davis, Toombs and the other leaders of the Southern junta in Congress issued an address approving the course of the seceders at Charleston, advising them to take no action at Richmond, but to await the result of the Baltimore Convention and expressing the conviction that, if fair concessions were not made to the South, other delegations would join them.

They accordingly came to Baltimore and demanded their seats in that Convention. But some of the States had elected new delegations which claimed them. For days confusion prevailed. Douglas sent two messages suggesting that his candidacy be dropped. But there were suppressed by his friends, who inexorably demanded his nomination. Five more States withdrew and the chairman resigned and joined the seceders. The Convention reorganized itself and proceeded to ballot. Douglas received all but thirteen votes; less, however, than the required two-thirds of all the delegates elected. But a resolution was passed declaring him nominated on the ground that he had received the votes of two-thirds of all delegates present. Senator Fitzpatrick of Alabama was nominated for Vice-President and the Convention adjourned. He declined and the Committee placed Herschel V. Johnson of Georgia in his place.

The seceders, joined by the recent recruits, held their Convention in Baltimore on the 28th of June and nominated John C. Breckenridge of Kentucky for President and Joseph Lane of Oregon for Vice-President.

This did not bring about a new condition, but revealed one which had existed for many years. The South was technically right in it demand that the Convention declare itself explicitly in favor of the honest and faithful maintenance of its constitutional rights in the Territories. These rights had been vehemently denied by the Republicans, but triumphantly established on a solid basis by the decision of the Supreme Court. Douglas had quibbled over the decision and explained it away until it seemed doubtful whether it in fact settled anything. The platform adopted by his supporters in the Convention recited the differences of opinion among Democrats as to the exact limits of the powers of the territorial legislature and those of Congress and referred the question again to the Court with a pledge to abide by its decision. They seemed to forget that the whole question had already been decided in the most sweeping terms in favor of the extreme Southern demands. It is not impossible that, had the South consented tot his vague and disingenuous platform and vigorously supported Douglas, he might have been elected. But "the South was implacable towards him and deliberately resolved to accept defeat rather than secure a victory under his lead."

The Republicans, meanwhile, had held their memorable Convention at Chicago, where, on May 18th, Lincoln had been nominated. When the news arrived in Washington, it made a great stir. The Republican Senators and Members gathered around Douglas to hear his judgement of the new statesman who had risen in the West.

"Gentlemen," he said, " you have nominated a very able and a very honest man."

On the adjournment of Congress, disregarding the decorous custom of seventy years, he entered the campaign, making speeches in his own behalf. He knew from the outset that with only a fraction of his party at his back, his chances of election were slight. But he fought on fiercely, partly from temperament and partly from conviction that he ought, if possible, to prevent Lincoln's election. Besides, there was a shadowy possibility of an election by the House of Representatives. At times his old Democratic enthusiasm returned. He told one audience that had his party given him undivided support he would have carried every State in the Union against Lincoln, except two.

He was sincerely alarmed for the safety of the Union in case of Lincoln's election, which he believed probable. He urged upon the South the duty of submitting to the result whatever it might be. At Norfolk, Virginia, he was asked whether, if Lincoln was elected, the Southern States would be justified in seceding from the Union?

To this he said, "I answer emphatically, No! The election of a man to the Presidency * * * in conformity with the Constitution * * * would not justify any attempt at dissolving this glorious Confederacy."

He further told them that if Lincoln were elected he would aid him to the extent of his power in maintaining the supremacy of the laws against all resistance to them from whatever quarter, and that it would be the President's duty to treat all attempts to break up the Union as Jackson treated the nullifiers in 1832. His candidacy was obviously hopeless. He exerted himself to avert the coming storm. Lincoln received one million eight hundred and sixty-seven thousand votes, Douglas one million two hundred and ninety-one thousand, and Brekenridge eight hundred and fifty thousand. Of the three hundred and three electoral votes Douglas received but twelve. Lincoln had an electoral majority over all opposing candidates.

On the 13th of November, South Carolina called a Convention to consider the dangers incident to her position in the Federal Union which, on December 20th, unanimously adopted an ordinance of secession. Three weeks later Mississippi declared herself out of the Union and was promptly followed by Florida, Alabama and Georgia. By the 20th of May eleven States had seceded. The President looked on it as a lawsuit between the States and exhausted his very respectable legal learning and ingenuity in proving that he had no power to raise his hand in defense of the country. It may be that the lawyer, with his quiddits and quillets, had survived the man. It may be that he had so long breathed the atmosphere of treason in the Cabinet counsels that he was tinctured with the widely prevalent pestilence. It is much more likely that the timorous old man, finding his term of office ending amid universal ruin, his friends and masters rushing into mad rebellion against his Government, weakly adopted that famous sentiment of the French King: "It will outlast my time."

Congress met on the third of December. In his message the President charged the entire trouble to the aggressive anti-slavery activity of the North, which had at last driven the South to open rebellion. He protested that he was powerless to act and referred the whole matter to Congress. Three of the Cabinet were serving the enemy and many seats in the House and Senate were held by unblushing traitors. The forts in Charleston harbor were besieged by South Carolina. The Government at first dared not and later could not relieve them.

Congress, if not as completely palsied as the President, was without remedy for the fearful evils of the time. Besides its quota of positive traitors, many of its members were infected with the mild, moonshiny political philosophy which had been currently in Washington for a quarter of a century. Many were about to retire to private life, and, like Buchanan, thought the Government would outlast their time. A famous Senate Committee of Thirteen, and a corresponding House Committee of Thirty-three, were appointed to consider the state of the Nation; both of which toiled much and accomplished nothing.

The Committee of Thirteen reported late in December that it was unable to agree, and on January 3rd Douglas addressed the Senate upon this report. He reviewed at great length the history of slavery legislation and drew from it all the conclusion that the trouble had arisen from unwarrantable interference in the local affairs of the Territories, and that, had popular sovereignty been given a chance it would have solved the problem long since and would do it yet if fairly tried. He ascribed the trouble to the pernicious agitation of the Republicans, and recalled Lincoln's most radical anti-slavery utterances in the famous campaign of 1858. He assured the people of the South that Lincoln would be powerless to hurt them if they remained in the Union, for there would be a majority against him in both the Houses of Congress. He denied utterly the right of South Carolina to secede and repudiate its constitutional duties, and insisted on the right of the Federal Government to enforce the law in all of the States. Yet, while there was a ray of hope, war must not be resorted to.

"In my opinion," he continued, "war is disunion, certain, inevitable, and irrevocable. * * * We have reached a point where disunion is inevitable unless some compromise, founded upon mutual concession, can be made. I prefer compromise to war. I prefer concession to a dissolution of the Union."

He asked the Republicans to consent to the reestablishment of the Missouri Compromise line, which he had swept away six years before amid their earnest protestations. He also proposed to establish popular sovereignty by constitutional amendment, such sovereignty to begin when a Territory had 50,000 inhabitants, and, by another amendment, to prohibit future acquisition of territory without a concurrent vote of two-thirds of each House of Congress. His purpose, he said, was not to settle the slavery question, but to expel slavery agitation from the arena of Federal politics forever.

This was his last important speech in the Senate. It was delivered under circumstances of awful solemnity. He seemed not deeply impressed with the gravity of the situation and was still interested in it chiefly as a party problem. He did not expect the baptism of blood that followed, but cheerfully looked forward to compromise and reconciliation. The Northern Democrats might yet rescue the country by mediating a truce between radical Republicans and radical Southern Democrats. In the present state of affairs who, but himself, the chief of these neutrals, could lead this great movement? His mental habits were those of the politician. He saw all event primarily in their relation to party tactics. Now that the earth began to rock beneath his feet, he suspected that it was only a theatrical earthquake and prepared to seize upon every advantage that might be gathered out of the confusion. He could not comprehend the deep and unappeasable passions that rent the Nation. The grim earnestness of his fellow-countrymen was as inconceivable to him as the demoniac enthusiasm of the great Apostle was to the scoffing Athenians who heard him on the Hill of Mars. But, as the great tragedy deepened and darkened, he quit his political speculations and began to think, not of the success of his party, but of the possibility of saving the Union from imminent wreck.

He returned to Illinois and addressed the legislature, urging energetic support of the war, and on May 1st was welcomed back to Chicago by an immense assembly of all parties. He was escorted to the great hall in which Lincoln had been nominated and there addressed the people. He spoke not as a politician but as a generous patriot. He denounced in unmeasured terms the Southern conspiracy which had resulted in secession and now had ripened into open and bloody rebellion. He saw the treason of the South no longer as a mere element in an interesting political game, but as the blackest of human crimes and an awful menace to the life of the Republic.

"There are only two sides to the question," he said. "Every man must be for the United States or against it. There can be no neutrals in this war; only patriots or traitors. * * * It is a sad task to discuss questions so fearful as civil war; but sad as it is, bloody and disastrous as I expect it will be, I express it as my conviction before God that it is the duty of every American citizen to rally around the flag of his country."

Not long after his return home he was stricken with serious sickness. The disease was not of such a character that it was expected to prove fatal, but the highest medical skill and most tender nursing were unavailing. The truth was, although unsuspected, that his vital energies were completely exhausted by the enormous labors and deep agitations of the past ten years. He had just passed his 48th birthday but was already gray and prematurely old. He had dwelt amid the tempest for twenty years and had felt more of severe strain than most men who had seen the Psalmist's three score years and ten. When told that his end was near, and asked what message he would send to his boys:

"Tell them," he said, "to obey the laws and support the Constitution of the United States."

On the morning of June 3rd he died. His remains lie buried in Chicago on the shore of Lake Michigan, a spot fitly chosen as the last resting place of this most ceaselessly active and inexhaustibly resourceful of American statesmen.

History has not been kind to Douglas. The farther we recede from events the more trivial seem the temporary circumstances which influence them and the clearer appear the changeless principles which ought to mold men's conduct. But to the eager, impetuous man of action, the temporary circumstances are apt to be of overmastering force. He was a practical man of action, whose course was generally guided by the accidental circumstances of the hour, rather than by fixed principles. His education was defective. He entered the great arena with little of either mental or moral culture. Yet, severely as we now judge him, he did not fall below the prevailing standard of political morals. His real sin was that he did not rise above the ethics of the times; that he remained deaf as an adder to the voices of the great reformers who sought to regenerate the age, and who were compelled to grapple with him in deadly struggle before they could gain footing on the stage. The time was out of joint and he felt no vocation to set it right. While his ethics has fared hard, his mental gifts have been over-estimated. The availability of all his resources, his overwhelming energy and marvelous efficiency among men of intellect, gave rise to the impression which still survives that he was a man of original genius. But of all his numerous speeches, heard or read by millions, not a sentence had enough vitality to survive even one generation. Though for ten years of stormy agitation he was the most commanding figure in our public life and wielded power of which Presidents and Cabinets stood in awe, the things for which he is chiefly remembered are his unfortunate doctrine of popular sovereignty and the resistless power with which he defended his most dubious relation to the question of slavery.

His powerful influence upon the overshadowing question of the times, his restless activity in shaping the course of great political events, fast drifting into darkest tragedy, have obscured his work in less conspicuous fields. While it does not come within the scope of this work to do more than portray his relation to the great national tragedy which was slowly evolving during the entire period of his political life, it should not be forgotten that his activity covered the whole field of legislation and that no man responded more generously or efficiently to the countless demands upon time and energy which so greatly burden the American statesman.

It is pleasant to find a Lieutenant General of the United States army in his old age and retirement recalling a visit in his boyhood to Washington, to seek redress of some West Point grievance, and how the only man he could find who had the leisure enough to effectively interview the Secretary of War on his behalf was Douglas.

It is sufficient for our purposes to say that for thirteen years he had practical control of all legislation affecting the Western Territories, that he drafted the bills establishing territorial governments for Minnesota, Kansas, Nebraska, Utah, New Mexico and Washington and prepared the acts for the admission of Wisconsin, California, Minnesota and Oregon. He secured for his State an enormous grant of public land, which resulted in the building of the Illinois Central Railroad. He warmly advocated the building of a railway to the Pacific. He consistently favored the most liberal appropriations for internal improvements, and, with that provincial patriotism and jealousy of Old World interference which was fashionable fifty years ago, vigorously opposed the Clayton-Bulwer treaty as a practical annulment of the Monroe doctrine.

It is not to be set down in his list of sins that he failed to bridge over the widening chasm between the North and the South; but it must be charged to him as a mental defect that he hopelessly failed to comprehend the significance of the great movements which he seemed to lead, that in the keenness of his interest in the evolutions of political strategy he failed to discern the symptoms of coming revolution.

When the storm that had been brewing before his eyes for ten years broke upon the country it took him by surprise. The ardor of his temperament, the eagerness of his ambition, make his conduct at times painfully resemble that of the selfish demagogue. But the range of his vision was small. He erred less from corruption of the heart than from deficiency of the mind. But what statesman of note during those strange and portentous years preceding the war could safely expose his speech and conduct to the searchlight of criticism? The wisest walked in darkness and stumbled often. It was not the fate of Douglas to see the mists amid which he had groped swept away by the hurricane of war.

What he would have done had his life been protracted ten year longer, is subject of interesting speculation. By temperament and habit he belonged to the preceding generation and it is difficult to conceive him working in harmony with the fiery and unyielding Puritans who succeeded. He loved the Union heartily and hated secession. He would have supported Lincoln in the great crisis. In the regenerated America, which rose from the fiery baptisms of the war, with its new ideal, its new hopes, its new convictions and deeper earnestness, he would probably have found himself sadly out of place. The epoch of history to which he belonged was closed. Young as he was, he had outlived his historic era and there is a dramatic fitness in the ending of his career at this time.

The Codes Of Hammurabi And Moses
W. W. Davies

QTY

The discovery of the Hammurabi Code is one of the greatest achievements of archaeology, and is of paramount interest, not only to the student of the Bible, but also to all those interested in ancient history...

Religion   **ISBN:** *1-59462-338-4*   **Pages:132**
MSRP $12.95

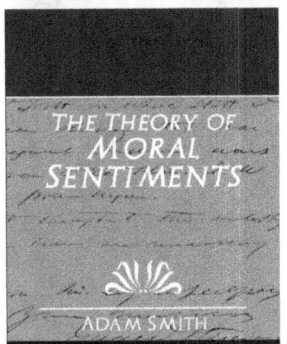

The Theory of Moral Sentiments
Adam Smith

QTY

This work from 1749. contains original theories of conscience amd moral judgment and it is the foundation for systemof morals.

Philosophy **ISBN:** *1-59462-777-0*   **Pages:536**
MSRP $19.95

Jessica's First Prayer
Hesba Stretton

QTY

In a screened and secluded corner of one of the many railway-bridges which span the streets of London there could be seen a few years ago, from five o'clock every morning until half past eight, a tidily set-out coffee-stall, consisting of a trestle and board, upon which stood two large tin cans, with a small fire of charcoal burning under each so as to keep the coffee boiling during the early hours of the morning when the work-people were thronging into the city on their way to their daily toil...

Childrens   **ISBN:** *1-59462-373-2*   **Pages:84**
MSRP $9.95

My Life and Work
Henry Ford

QTY

Henry Ford revolutionized the world with his implementation of mass production for the Model T automobile. Gain valuable business insight into his life and work with his own auto-biography... "We have only started on our development of our country we have not as yet, with all our talk of wonderful progress, done more than scratch the surface. The progress has been wonderful enough but..."

Biographies/   **ISBN:** *1-59462-198-5*   **Pages:300**
MSRP $21.95

The Art of Cross-Examination
Francis Wellman

QTY

I presume it is the experience of every author, after his first book is published upon an important subject, to be almost overwhelmed with a wealth of ideas and illustrations which could readily have been included in his book, and which to his own mind, at least, seem to make a second edition inevitable. Such certainly was the case with me; and when the first edition had reached its sixth impression in five months, I rejoiced to learn that it seemed to my publishers that the book had met with a sufficiently favorable reception to justify a second and considerably enlarged edition. ..

Pages:412

Reference   **ISBN:** *1-59462-647-2*   *MSRP $19.95*

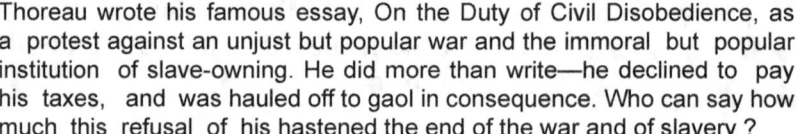

On the Duty of Civil Disobedience
Henry David Thoreau

QTY

Thoreau wrote his famous essay, On the Duty of Civil Disobedience, as a protest against an unjust but popular war and the immoral but popular institution of slave-owning. He did more than write—he declined to pay his taxes, and was hauled off to gaol in consequence. Who can say how much this refusal of his hastened the end of the war and of slavery ?

Law   **ISBN:** *1-59462-747-9*   **Pages:48**
MSRP $7.45

Dream Psychology Psychoanalysis for Beginners
Sigmund Freud

QTY

Sigmund Freud, born Sigismund Schlomo Freud (May 6, 1856 - September 23, 1939), was a Jewish-Austrian neurologist and psychiatrist who co-founded the psychoanalytic school of psychology. Freud is best known for his theories of the unconscious mind, especially involving the mechanism of repression; his redefinition of sexual desire as mobile and directed towards a wide variety of objects; and his therapeutic techniques, especially his understanding of transference in the therapeutic relationship and the presumed value of dreams as sources of insight into unconscious desires.

Pages:196

Psychology   **ISBN:** *1-59462-905-6*   *MSRP $15.45*

The Miracle of Right Thought
Orison Swett Marden

QTY

Believe with all of your heart that you will do what you were made to do. When the mind has once formed the habit of holding cheerful, happy, prosperous pictures, it will not be easy to form the opposite habit. It does not matter how improbable or how far away this realization may see, or how dark the prospects may be, if we visualize them as best we can, as vividly as possible, hold tenaciously to them and vigorously struggle to attain them, they will gradually become actualized, realized in the life. But a desire, a longing without endeavor, a yearning abandoned or held indifferently will vanish without realization.

Pages:360

Self Help   **ISBN:** *1-59462-644-8*   *MSRP $25.45*

www.bookjungle.com *email: sales@bookjungle.com fax: 630-214-0564 mail: Book Jungle PO Box 2226 Champaign, IL 61825*

QTY

☐ **The Rosicrucian Cosmo-Conception Mystic Christianity** *by Max Heindel* ISBN: *1-59462-188-8* **$38.95**
The Rosicrucian Cosmo-conception is not dogmatic, neither does it appeal to any other authority than the reason of the student. It is: not controversial, but is; sent forth in the, hope that it may help to clear... New Age/Religion Pages 646

☐ **Abandonment To Divine Providence** *by Jean-Pierre de Caussade* ISBN: *1-59462-228-0* **$25.95**
"The Rev. Jean Pierre de Caussade was one of the most remarkable spiritual writers of the Society of Jesus in France in the 18th Century. His death took place at Toulouse in 1751. His works have gone through many editions and have been republished... Inspirational/Religion Pages 400

☐ **Mental Chemistry** *by Charles Haanel* ISBN: *1-59462-192-6* **$23.95**
Mental Chemistry allows the change of material conditions by combining and appropriately utilizing the power of the mind. Much like applied chemistry creates something new and unique out of careful combinations of chemicals the mastery of mental chemistry... New Age Pages 354

☐ **The Letters of Robert Browning and Elizabeth Barret Barrett 1845-1846 vol II** ISBN: *1-59462-193-4* **$35.95**
by Robert Browning and Elizabeth Barrett Biographies Pages 596

☐ **Gleanings In Genesis (volume I)** *by Arthur W. Pink* ISBN: *1-59462-130-6* **$27.45**
Appropriately has Genesis been termed "the seed plot of the Bible" for in it we have, in germ form, almost all of the great doctrines which are afterwards fully developed in the books of Scripture which follow... Religion/Inspirational Pages 420

☐ **The Master Key** *by L. W. de Laurence* ISBN: *1-59462-001-6* **$30.95**
In no branch of human knowledge has there been a more lively increase of the spirit of research during the past few years than in the study of Psychology, Concentration and Mental Discipline. The requests for authentic lessons in Thought Control, Mental Discipline and... New Age/Business Pages 422

☐ **The Lesser Key Of Solomon Goetia** *by L. W. de Laurence* ISBN: *1-59462-092-X* **$9.95**
This translation of the first book of the "Lernegton" which is now for the first time made accessible to students of Talismanic Magic was done, after careful collation and edition, from numerous Ancient Manuscripts in Hebrew, Latin, and French... New Age/Occult Pages 92

☐ **Rubaiyat Of Omar Khayyam** *by Edward Fitzgerald* ISBN:*1-59462-332-5* **$13.95**
Edward Fitzgerald, whom the world has already learned, in spite of his own efforts to remain within the shadow of anonymity, to look upon as one of the rarest poets of the century, was born at Bredfield, in Suffolk, on the 31st of March, 1809. He was the third son of John Purcell... Music Pages 172

☐ **Ancient Law** *by Henry Maine* ISBN: *1-59462-128-4* **$29.95**
The chief object of the following pages is to indicate some of the earliest ideas of mankind, as they are reflected in Ancient Law, and to point out the relation of those ideas to modern thought. Religion/History Pages 452

☐ **Far-Away Stories** *by William J. Locke* ISBN: *1-59462-129-2* **$19.45**
"Good wine needs no bush, but a collection of mixed vintages does. And this book is just such a collection. Some of the stories I do not want to remain buried for ever in the museum files of dead magazine-numbers an author's not unpardonable vanity..." Fiction Pages 272

☐ **Life of David Crockett** *by David Crockett* ISBN: *1-59462-250-7* **$27.45**
"Colonel David Crockett was one of the most remarkable men of the times in which he lived. Born in humble life, but gifted with a strong will, an indomitable courage, and unremitting perseverance... Biographies/New Age Pages 424

☐ **Lip-Reading** *by Edward Nitchie* ISBN: *1-59462-206-X* **$25.95**
Edward B. Nitchie, founder of the New York School for the Hard of Hearing, now the Nitchie School of Lip-Reading, Inc, wrote "LIP-READING Principles and Practice". The development and perfecting of this meritorious work on lip-reading was an undertaking... How-to Pages 400

☐ **A Handbook of Suggestive Therapeutics, Applied Hypnotism, Psychic Science** ISBN: *1-59462-214-0* **$24.95**
by Henry Munro Health/New Age/Health/Self-help Pages 376

☐ **A Doll's House: and Two Other Plays** *by Henrik Ibsen* ISBN: *1-59462-112-8* **$19.95**
Henrik Ibsen created this classic when in revolutionary 1848 Rome. Introducing some striking concepts in playwriting for the realist genre, this play has been studied the world over. Fiction/Classics/Plays 308

☐ **The Light of Asia** *by sir Edwin Arnold* ISBN: *1-59462-204-3* **$13.95**
In this poetic masterpiece, Edwin Arnold describes the life and teachings of Buddha. The man who was to become known as Buddha to the world was born as Prince Gautama of India but he rejected the worldly riches and abandoned the reigns of power when... Religion/History/Biographies Pages 170

☐ **The Complete Works of Guy de Maupassant** *by Guy de Maupassant* ISBN: *1-59462-157-8* **$16.95**
"For days and days, nights and nights, I had dreamed of that first kiss which was to consecrate our engagement, and I knew not on what spot I should put my lips..." Fiction/Classics Pages 240

☐ **The Art of Cross-Examination** *by Francis L. Wellman* ISBN: *1-59462-309-0* **$26.95**
Written by a renowned trial lawyer, Wellman imparts his experience and uses case studies to explain how to use psychology to extract desired information through questioning. How-to/Science/Reference Pages 408

☐ **Answered or Unanswered?** *by Louisa Vaughan* ISBN: *1-59462-248-5* **$10.95**
Miracles of Faith in China Religion Pages 112

☐ **The Edinburgh Lectures on Mental Science (1909)** *by Thomas* ISBN: *1-59462-008-3* **$11.95**
This book contains the substance of a course of lectures recently given by the writer in the Queen Street Hall, Edinburgh. Its purpose is to indicate the Natural Principles governing the relation between Mental Action and Material Conditions... New Age/Psychology Pages 148

☐ **Ayesha** *by H. Rider Haggard* ISBN: *1-59462-301-5* **$24.95**
Verily and indeed it is the unexpected that happens! Probably if there was one person upon the earth from whom the Editor of this, and of a certain previous history, did not expect to hear again... Classics Pages 380

☐ **Ayala's Angel** *by Anthony Trollope* ISBN: *1-59462-352-X* **$29.95**
The two girls were both pretty, but Lucy who was twenty-one who supposed to be simple and comparatively unattractive, whereas Ayala was credited, as her Bombwhat romantic name might show, with poetic charm and a taste for romance. Ayala when her father died was nineteen... Fiction Pages 484

☐ **The American Commonwealth** *by James Bryce* ISBN: *1-59462-286-8* **$34.45**
An interpretation of American democratic political theory. It examines political mechanics and society from the perspective of Scotsman James Bryce Politics Pages 572

☐ **Stories of the Pilgrims** *by Margaret P. Pumphrey* ISBN: *1-59462-116-0* **$17.95**
This book explores pilgrims religious oppression in England as well as their escape to Holland and eventual crossing to America on the Mayflower, and their early days in New England... History Pages 268

QTY

The Fasting Cure *by Sinclair Upton*   ISBN: *1-59462-222-1* **$13.95**

In the Cosmopolitan Magazine for May, 1910, and in the Contemporary Review (London) for April, 1910, I published an article dealing with my experiences in fasting. I have written a great many magazine articles, but never one which attracted so much attention... New Age/Self Help/Health Pages 164

Hebrew Astrology *by Sepharial*   ISBN: *1-59462-308-2* **$13.45**

In these days of advanced thinking it is a matter of common observation that we have left many of the old landmarks behind and that we are now pressing forward to greater heights and to a wider horizon than that which represented the mind-content of our progenitors... Astrology Pages 144

Thought Vibration or The Law of Attraction in the Thought World   ISBN: *1-59462-127-6* **$12.95**

by William Walker Atkinson   Psychology/Religion Pages 144

Optimism *by Helen Keller*   ISBN: *1-59462-108-X* **$15.95**

Helen Keller was blind, deaf, and mute since 19 months old, yet famously learned how to overcome these handicaps, communicate with the world, and spread her lectures promoting optimism. An inspiring read for everyone... Biographies/Inspirational Pages 84

Sara Crewe *by Frances Burnett*   ISBN: *1-59462-360-0* **$9.45**

In the first place, Miss Minchin lived in London. Her home was a large, dull, tall one, in a large, dull square, where all the houses were alike, and all the sparrows were alike, and where all the door-knockers made the same heavy sound... Childrens/Classic Pages 88

The Autobiography of Benjamin Franklin *by Benjamin Franklin*   ISBN: *1-59462-135-7* **$24.95**

The Autobiography of Benjamin Franklin has probably been more extensively read than any other American historical work, and no other book of its kind has had such ups and downs of fortune. Franklin lived for many years in England, where he was agent... Biographies/History Pages 332

Name	
Email	
Telephone	
Address	
City, State ZIP	

☐ **Credit Card**   ☐ **Check / Money Order**

Credit Card Number	
Expiration Date	
Signature	

Please Mail to: Book Jungle
PO Box 2226
Champaign, IL 61825
or Fax to: 630-214-0564

ORDERING INFORMATION

web: *www.bookjungle.com*
email: *sales@bookjungle.com*
fax: *630-214-0564*
mail: *Book Jungle PO Box 2226 Champaign, IL 61825*
or PayPal *to sales@bookjungle.com*

Please contact us for bulk discounts

DIRECT-ORDER TERMS

**20% Discount if You Order
Two or More Books**
Free Domestic Shipping!
Accepted: Master Card, Visa,
Discover, American Express